The blackfish swept back along the netting, looking up at us again.

I got my first good, close view of him. His throat and belly were alabaster white, and the white circled up, as if painted on, over his sides and back, which was the color of wet charcoal. Another oval of white sat above and just behind his eyes. His round snout was interrupted with those two rows of conical teeth, spaced alternately so they could interlock. An eating machine was what we faced.

Papa said, "Wow," and stood up, making his way around the pilothouse to pick up the CB microphone and call repeatedly for Mama. In a moment she came on. Papa asked cleverly, "Honey, you wanna go to Maui? Over."

Mama answered laughingly, "Why are you calling me to ask that? You just left here. Why didn't you ask me then? Sure, I want to go to Maui."

Papa said, "Well, we jus' got the ticket. Jamie and I trapped that big buster blackfish up here at Wilwilli Cove. Got him right in the bottle."

Mama laughed again. "I don't believe you, Perry Tidd."

"We got him, all right. I swear to it! Jamie, yell to your mother that we got the blackfish."

I did.

THEODORE TAYLOR is the author of many books, among them *The Cay*, which won eleven literary awards, including the Lewis Carroll Shelf Award, *Tora! Tora! Tora!*, and *Walking Up a Rainbow*. He lives in Laguna Beach, California.

NORTHWESTERN U.S.A. and CANADIAN BORDER

BRITISH COLUMBIA
PORT HARDY
VANCOUVER
Vancouver Island
SEATTLE
WASHINGTON
PORTLAND
OREGON

COASTAL BRITISH COLUMBIA

CALVERT ISLAND
PORT HARDY
VANCOUVER
Vancouver Island

PORT HARDY VICINITY

LUMBER LANDING
CALVERT ISLAND
PORT HARDY
Vancouver Island

WILWILLI COVE • LUMBER LANDING

WILWILLI CREEK
WILWILLI COVE
NORTH ROCK
SOUTH ROCK
COTTAGES
OLD CANNERY
LUMBER RIVER
FLOATS
BOATS
FITZ HUGH SOUND
(INSIDE PASSAGE)
PRINCE RUPERT and ALASKA
BUY BARGE PORT HARDY

The Hostage

THEODORE TAYLOR

LAUREL-LEAF BOOKS

Published by
Dell Publishing
a division of
Bantam Doubleday Dell Publishing Group, Inc.
1540 Broadway
New York, New York 10036

The trademark Laurel-Leaf Library® is registered in the U.S. Patent and Trademark Office.

The trademark Dell® is registered in the U.S. Patent and Trademark Office.

ISBN :0-440-20923-4

RL: 6.5

Reprinted by arrangement with Delacorte Press

Printed in the United States of America

August 1991

10 9 8 7

RAD

For my son, Mark, with love

ACKNOWLEDGMENT

I would like to thank the following for their technical advice and assistance: Dr. Marilyn T. Dahlheim, National Marine Mammal Laboratory, Seattle, Washington; Major James McBean, Transport and Rescue Squadron RCC 442, Comox, Vancouver Island, B.C.; Clifford Todd, Fisheries and Oceans, Victoria, B.C.; David Knapton, Fisheries and Oceans, Prince Rupert, B.C.; Captain David Harding, troller, Gibson, B.C.; Captain Mark Taylor, San Diego, California.

THE WORLD
OF THE KILLER WHALE

*T*here was poetry to the killer whale's world as he swam along, gliding just beneath the surface or rising and falling in the thin band of light. Sky. Wind and sea. A lovely free loneliness. Sailors always found this hard to put into words but he didn't bother. It was his home—the gliding upward to breathe, surfacing, the slight dive, flukes up and dripping to send him down again. Each move rhythmical, rolling on, trailing bubbles. Desdemona and Persephone, his lovers, were off on his starboard side, swimming easily.

Ahead might be a few days of sun. Then other days when the clouds met the sea. Violent storms did not particularly affect him. Going was easier in calm weather but beneath the surface it was much the same. Whether he rose to breathe in the trough of a wave or on the crest of it, the procedure was the same. His breathing valve closed when he dived. Of course the machine-gunning of rain or sleet added a little more static to the cacophony beneath the waves.

But storms were a part of life, for either fisherman or killer whale.

He had only one deadly enemy.

THEODORE TAYLOR
Laguna Beach, California

1

January: We got to the South Pointers just before daylight and already there were spits of snow in the air. The North Pacific sky was dark and boiling, almost black, and the wind was picking up, icy cold, from the southwest. There'd been nothing but bad news on the Coast Guard weather channel since we left Lumber Landing. Using our single side-band radio, Papa had been monitoring Vancouver on the hour. We'd also listened to that lady from Kodiak, Peggy Dyson, WBH 20, who broadcasts weather conditions from the Bering Sea clear down to Seattle.

About noon, with about eighty measly dollars in fish aboard, Papa said, "We'll go pretty soon."

I was hoping we would. I had an uneasy feeling.

By one o'clock the seas were hissing by, higher than our wheelhouse. They had an ugly slate-gray color and the tops were already beginning to blow, like a white fringe. The wind was starting to hum.

Papa, looking around, said, "Okay, let's pull the plug and start home." We battened down and secured all the hatches, lashed the gear on the afterdeck of our gillnetter-troller.

I was relieved but the entrance to Hakai Passage, the beginning of sheltered water, was still eighteen miles away and the *Dawn Girl* would be at the mercy of open ocean for well more than two hours.

Hanging on as she pitched and tossed and lurched, I stood silently by Papa in the wheelhouse as we cranked up and headed northeast.

Window wipers labored as the snow began to thicken and soon visibility was less than a hundred feet. Seas were dwarfing us, rolling behind us, chasing us, lifting the stern as if it were thistle, then letting us slide down the hill of white-topped water, burying the bow. Then we'd stagger up the next high hill, shaking off foam.

If the engine was flooded, or failed for any other reason, we wouldn't have a chance. The *Dawn Girl* would swing sideways in the trough and over we'd go.

Papa's face was grim as he grasped the wheel, steering the boat, worried more about getting swamped in the stern than what was ahead of us. Freak waves, giants forty or fifty feet high, were always a worry in any gale. I'd never seen him frightened before. He was now, and that alone terrified me.

I saw him reach down to the locker that was a few feet away from the wheel, on the starboard side. His fingers made sure the latch was free. In that locker were two survival suits. They looked like space suits that the first astronauts wore. Locking out freezing water, keeping body heat in, they could keep you alive for hours in the wildest sea.

Soon, Papa said, as calmly as he could, "Jamie, why don't you put one on, just for the heck of it. You haven't tried one since we bought 'em." Neither had he.

I wriggled into that orange-colored plastic skin, with its built-in hood, boots, and gloves, happy to be in its warmth. Those suits had already saved hundreds of fishermen in north waters. Then he put his own on.

The radio was full of static, fading in and out, but there was a boat to the north of us in deep trouble, calling urgently for help, pleading with anyone in the vicinity to rush to her estimated position. Dead in the water, her engine gone, she was sixty miles from the nearest Coast Guard cutter. Then she went silent.

Papa said, "She needs praying for."

So did we, a moment later.

A giant following sea caught us and curled over us, and for a few seconds we were completely trapped underwater like we were inside a submarine. I thought that the engine had stopped, or missed a beat, the exhaust stack filling up with sea. It got quiet, it seemed.

Then we came out of it, the *Dawn Girl* shaking off the knockout blow, water spilling from the wheelhouse roof and down the deck. We rose up and climbed another hill, then slid sideways as the Volvo roared again. Thank God that engine was new.

Papa breathed out, "Boy, you'll never come closer to death than that."

About an hour later we made it to Hakai Passage and the seas flattened out.

Papa got on the CB to tell Mama we were safe and in the passage, heading for the buy barge with our small catch of bottom fish, and then on home.

2

The last fierce storm, carrying a lot of cold driving rain, hit us at Lumber Landing in mid-April. Yet it didn't stop McCoy's boat from edging up to the float to dump off mailbags, some crates and boxes, and two passengers.

I remember that Cap'n Selby, who'd been down at Port Hardy, on Vancouver Island, having his dentures fixed, hobbled off the *Nootka*, water streaming from his hat. He was yelling at me cheerfully, "Jamie, watch you don't get wet." Cap'n Selby always thought he said funny things. They were usually dumb. Not funny at all.

"Try not to, Cap'n," I yelled back.

Sticking his head out of the *Nootka*'s wheelhouse door, Farley McCoy, the skipper, shouted, "Hey, Jamie, tell your papa he was a dollar-ten short on that big envelope he sent to Vancouver last month. I'll collect next time I come."

I shouted back I'd do just that, grabbing the plastic bag marked "Tidds." Then I ran on up to the house, ducking the thirty-knot wind. In that spattered blue sack was three weeks' worth of letters, magazines, advertisements, and a reminder from the rotten bank that payment was due on Papa's new engine and nets. I was hoping, of course, that some would be addressed to me, James Wilson Tidd.

After I distributed everything, we all settled down to read. Next to having a full boatload of salmon or an angel telling us someone had just died and left us a tax-free million, mail-time was the best time of all. Bills were always last in the order of opening.

No letter from Angie Pinheiro, my "girlfriend," up in Prince Rupert.

Papa soon whistled softly and let go a curious kind of laugh. "Now, would you look at this? They got to be kiddin'. A hundred thousand, U.S., for a big blackfish. Someone's lost their mind."

On my belly on a big braided oval rug Mama had made, I looked up from the linoleum floor. A hundred thousand for a blackfish. April Fool! I laughed too.

Mama stopped thumbing through a catalog from an expensive department store in Victoria, one she couldn't afford. She also knew the prices of what swam in the sea.

Killer whales, which we called blackfish, often roamed the inland waters of British Columbia, which was just "B.C." to us, coming up into our Fitz Hugh Sound, down by Cape Calvert, or going through Hakai Passage or up at Lama Passage. A pod, a family, always hung around the Queen Charlotte Strait, north of us.

They had an appetite for salmon, and fishing people don't want anyone to eat fish except humans. But they also had an appetite for sea lions, which really gobbled salmon, and that was all right with us too. So there was bad and good about blackfish. I'd thrown rocks at them from the sea cliff. They were as familiar as eagles or the north wind. Nothing to get excited about.

Papa said, "I don't think many have been trapped in the last ten years. Those Greenpeace people chase that boat from Sealand every time it goes after them in Barkley Sound."

Barkley Sound is on the west coast of Vancouver Island, near Ucluelet.

At that particular moment we were in the kitchen of our two-bedroom white house. Actually, the "white" was pretty dingy, streaked with brown splotches from the mean weather. Cooking room, dining room, living room, talk room, recreation room, workroom—the only constantly warm room in the house.

In better days Papa had bought a lot of expensive work clothes and on wooden pegs on the north wall hung yellow Helly-Hansen foul-weather gear; below were black fleece-lined rubber boots, a pair for each of us. Polypropylene long johns and thermal socks often draped Mama's drying rack in winter and spring. Fishing gear might be in any corner on any day. Coils of steel wire. Salmon trolling spoons. Nets were repaired in that room. The CB, the citizen's band radio, so that Mama and Papa could talk back and forth when we were at sea, when we were in range, had an important corner. We lived in that room, except to sleep, and if the world suddenly blew up, we'd certainly die there too.

That cottage, and I well remember every splintery cedar inch of it, sat in a clearing surrounded by tall timber, overlooking the little harbor. At the time only nine of the eighteen houses, arranged like soldiers in three rows near the rotting old cannery, were occupied.

Once there'd been bunkhouses for Chinese workers, while the Swedes, Norwegians, Finns, and Scots lived in the cottages. Shacks, up on pilings, in which poor Owikeno Indian workers and their families had lived, were collapsing. The big cannery had been abandoned forty years before. Lumber Landing was indeed a meager place.

As for people, there were almost as many dogs and cats as humans. The wintertime population was seven families—five Canadian, like us, one American, the Tito Debars, and the Pinheiros. A total of thirty-two men, women, and children plus the animals. During the summer salmon runs, fishing bachelors swelled the population by eight or ten, tying up at the floats. All the children stuck in this prison during winter were little, except me. So I had a problem to keep from going insane. I didn't always succeed.

From our kitchen window we could see the harbor, the eight boats that usually operated from it, and then the deep waters of Fitz Hugh, often checkered with driftwood. On a clear day, which was seldom, we could see Hecate and Nalau islands; on clear nights, the friendly flashing light on Kelpie Point, about three and a half miles across Fitz Hugh.

Of course there was always that parade of ships and boats, particularly in summer, up and down the Inside Passage to the B.C. coastal villages and Alaska. They were comforting sights, reducing loneliness, when they could be seen.

"Every boat in the whole godforsaken fishery'll be on the hunt for blacks, me included," said Papa, excited. "Sure wish I could check this figure. Maybe they meant ten thousand. Even so, I'll take it. Would I ever?"

"Who needs a blackfish?" asked Mama.

"Some new ocean park in Southern California, you might know. All those people down there want the biggest of everythin'. And that is what is goin' to separate the sharks from the minnies, as they say. Imagine gettin' alongside a twenty-five-foot black an' sayin', 'Hey, buddy, come on into my net.' "

Mama frowned again. "That's only seven feet shorter'n the *Dawn Girl.*" We used her for both gillnetting and trolling.

Gillnetting is a wall of nylon netting floating out from the boat. How you catch the individual fish depends on the size and shape. Fish sticks his head into the net and then is caught by the gill covers or some get tangled into the webs with their fins or snouts or even their scales. Nothing much to it providing fish are around. The boat drifts and the net drifts with it. Trolling is dragging flashing lures, usually silver-colored spoons, with hooks attached, through the water. Good way to catch big salmon.

"Why, yes, it is only seven feet shorter," Papa said. He then half grunted and half laughed and I could guess that he was thinking about taking on that much fish. Why, the blacks had power enough to tow the *Dawn Girl* around like it was a wood chip. One bash and they could stove it in, making us swim in icy water.

I glanced at the ad.

WANTED—KILLER WHALE *(Orcinus orca)*—Will pay $100,000 for a killer whale in good condition. Must be twenty-five feet or over. Call Zachary Cooke, Ocean Arena, Sea Shows, Inc., Huntington Beach, California. 1-800-003-1002.

"A hundred thousand for an old blackfish? I can't believe it," I said.

Papa laughed. "That's what I just said."

"Get us one, Papa!" I dropped back to the magazine, eyes greeting a Suzuki flaring out on a hill, spinning clouds of dust.

My long-legged mother, in faded jeans and a plaid Pendleton shirt, stepped around the ancient oblong wooden stove and over to the pink Formica table, glancing down. The classified was in *The National Fisherman*, an oversized monthly that covered fisheries from Nova Scotia to Dutch Harbor, up in the Aleutians, shrimpers in the Gulf of Mexico, and tuna clippers in the South Pacific.

"Yeah," Mama agreed. "Do that, Per. Do it!"

There was no doubt at all about how she felt. What Mama exactly wanted him to do was sell the boat for whatever he could get and go back to civilization. She also wanted Papa to do something else to make a living. Work construction. Cut timber. Work anything but the boats. January was still on her mind. Only last week she'd said to me, "Every time you two go out, I wonder if it'll be the last time I see you." Well, she'd said that before.

Mama had lost her first husband, as a bride of nineteen, to a storm off Oregon. She'd sworn she'd never marry another fisherman, but then she'd met Canadian Perry Tidd in a Seattle cocktail lounge where she was a waitress in long stockings, short-shorts, and a low-cut blouse.

One night during the winter I'd heard them talking about the lack of money and going back to Vancouver and she'd said, "I don't mind going back to the lounge —funny, skinny Lacy in her short-shorts." But then she'd started to cry.

I looked quite a lot like her at the time. Same round face and brown eyes. Dark hair like hers, tending to curl. I was destined to be thin and lanky like her when I grew up.

I was a little over fourteen that interesting spring.

3

*P*apa's finger kept tapping at the block of type as he thought about the meaning of that ad. His hands were huge and scarred from hooks and fins. Most of his left index finger was missing, victim of a steel wire one day while trolling. There was no way to save the finger, so he simply threw it overboard.

"Ocean Arena," said Mama, thoughtfully. "That's like that Sea World place down in San Diego, I bet. Or like the place in Victoria. I went there when it first opened."

That was Sealand, on Vancouver Island.

"Coupla years ago that Sea World place applied to the U.S. government to trap a hundred blackfish an' got all kinds of hell. Greenpeace got after 'em good," said Papa.

Mama said, "Those Greenpeace people can give everybody fits."

They were the environmentalists, I knew, fighting against seal killers and whale killers, protecting all sea life.

Though she was still pretty at the age of thirty-five, my mother wore a definite tiredness around her eyes most of the time. Mental tiredness rather than physical tiredness. The remoteness of Lumber Landing, the usually bleak weather, the danger at sea, the financial struggle were wearing her down.

"Amen," Papa answered vaguely, thinking more about how to trap a six- or seven-ton blackfish than about Greenpeace. "You know, it's been done before, an' not too far from here. . . ."

I rolled over on my back, surprised. "Somebody like us got a blackfish near here?"

"Twenty years ago. Bill Lechkobit an' Bob McGarvey got eight thousand for one at Namu. Then Cecil Reid an' two more got twenty thousand for a whole pod down at Garden Bay. They weren't very big. Now, this California fellow wants the grandpop of all. So far as I know, there's still no law against taking 'em."

I stared at the rain slashing at the window, streaming down the glass, thinking what it would mean to us to have that much money. It went far beyond dirt bikes. Maybe farewell to the mental ward at Lumber Landing. Good Lord.

Winter before last and the one before that I'd spent in Port Hardy, a town to the south, at the end of Vancouver Island, going to school. But this year there hadn't been enough money to pay the board bill so I had to be content with Migrant Education Program courses mailed up from Victoria every month. On days that Papa didn't go fishing, and cut wood instead, I worked on the courses, hating every minute of it. There was electricity and fun and laughter in Point Hardy, small as it was.

Mama said, "Well, I'd settle for just three thousand of that. Just enough to take us all to Maui for three weeks. Oh, Lordy, would I! Sweet, warm Maui. Yukaloo."

She'd fastened on Maui, a place to which she'd never been, as an island that would take care of all her tiredness. Her body longed for hot sand.

I rolled over on the rug. I said, "I'll settle for this and school in Prince Rupert this fall." I tapped a page of *Dirt Rider*, which was also in the mailbag, gift from my grandpa down in Sacramento. Since I had nothing to ride off-road around Lumber Landing, the magazine was more or less an infuriating gift. Shining Husqvarnas, Kawasakis, Suzukis, Yamahas, and Hondas, breathing fire from slick pages, made me angry. My eyes ate up the Fox racing boots, the vented racing pants, Arai helmets and kidney belts and chest protectors. Sometimes I could almost hear the exhausts exploding in the dust, see the machines vaulting over a hill.

I wanted to sit my bony haunch in a saddle so bad that I ached. All for naught at Lumber Landing. There was no dust. No bike hills. Just leaf-mold trails through the silent woods, some so narrow that handlebars would jam.

Finger tapping on a Kawasaki KDX200A3, I read to them, "The KDX packs a power pulling 193cc, reed-valve single engine with six-speed tranny . . ."

Mama laughed and reached down to ruffle my hair. "I don't know what you're talking about, but I'll add that KDX to our shopping list."

"Yeah, add it on," Papa chuckled.

That ad had changed the whole atmosphere in the kitchen. Before the mail arrived there'd been enough gloom in there to reach Ketchikan.

The spring herring-roe fishery, just ended, hadn't

been successful, and now Papa was looking to the chinooks and summer sockeye runs to make this year. As an independent small-boat operator selling to the cooperative, the chances of ever being rich were slim but there was always hope. Or so he thought. "A couple good years an' we'll move to Prince Rupert, buy a new boat . . ."

Whether or not Mama agreed, fishing was all that he knew how to do, could do. He often cursed it but there was no other way of life for him. Mama was stuck with it, or leave him. I'm sure she'd thought about that at the Landing now and then. Leaving him.

We all three fell silent for a moment, just thinking about that much money, the muffled sound of the weather and a clock tick taking over. Rain cut laterally at the cottage, coming on the edge of the wind. That late spring storm was in its second day, and even Papa, with his reputation of being the original Viking, was glad to be in the cozy warmth of the house, not pounding around at sea. So was I. Mixed in with the rain was spindrift, flying spray, blowing off the sound, and the cottage, on the ocean side, would glitter with salt whenever the sun returned.

There was never much sun in the winter, and not even a lot of it in the summer, but the fjords and islands of the coast were beautiful, I'll have to admit. Mist did not hide this rugged beauty. The green mountains were stepped up, rank upon rank, to the snowtops. Along the shores, the firs, cedars, spruces, and hemlocks of the rain forest shimmered when the sun was out. It was grizzly bear and wolf and wolverine country, deer and raccoon country. Salmon country. Not people country.

Bald eagles sat in the trees on the islands, their

heads white knobs against the green. Ospreys soared on the wind. Humpback and killer-whale country. Remote, untamed shore country with air so clear and clean that not even fragrant woodsmoke could tarnish it for long. I was aware of all this but would gladly trade it on most days for the lights of Port Hardy or Prince Rupert.

Still musing, Papa finally said, "Seein' blackfish an' gettin' 'em are two different things. I'd never try to net one, even if I could. What would I do with it? Tow it in? Well, mebbe. It would likely drown. An' you can't stick a regular harpoon in a blackfish. Likely bleed it to death 'fore you ever got it in."

I sat up and looked at Papa, my imagination suddenly stirring. "How'd they do it at Namu?"

"Jus' got lucky, Jamie. Plain lucky. But I think this guy Zachary Cooke, whoever he is, may have to wait a long time for a twenty-five-foot blackfish."

Outside, the wind and rain roared on, gusting, shaking the cottage, reminding Mama, I think, of that awful January day and the trip back from South Pointers. She glanced over at the windward wall, fear of the storm and sea plainly in her eyes.

4

Then it was misty summer, early June, and the deHavilland Beaver float plane from Prince Rupert landed offshore after circling low a couple of times, winding on around into the harbor, destroying the Lumber Landing silence with its engine drone. Roosting gulls took off. Cottage doors opened that morning.

Angela Ione Pinheiro had come home after surviving her second year in high school. Or maybe it was the high school that had survived. The principal probably didn't have her IQ. I know he didn't have her talent for creating trouble.

The whole village, us three Tidds included, emptied down to the float while her papa, Cristo Pinheiro, paddled the family skiff out to take her off. Engine cut, the door opened, and there she was, grinning and waving like she was the Queen of England and we were all her loyal subjects. I had an idea she'd like that role, the Queen.

Everyone was yelling "Hi, Angie," or "Welcome home, Angie," and even the dogs were barking because of the excitement.

Her Highness disappeared back into the plane for a moment while the pilot unloaded her baggage into Cristo's boat. It looked like she had enough to last a lifetime.

I said to Mama, "That's more than what she had last September."

I got a look back that said, Certainly, you idiot. She's been gone nine months! Women shop.

Papa just shrugged.

I now must admit I couldn't have been happier that June day, though she was a year older than I was and sometimes held it against me. Most of what we had in common, aside from working the fishing boats, was the fact that I was the only boy there anywhere near her age, and vice versa. She was somebody less than wrinkled thirty, or older than five, that I could talk to and that was like a celebration to me. Vice versa to that, too, I think.

Then she climbed out onto the float and everybody crowded around her, except me. I hung back, on purpose. I watched.

After they all had their turn, hugging and kissing and rattling away, I stepped over.

"Hey, Jamie, how you doin'?" was the first spectacular thing she said to me, kissing my cheek, giving me a pretty good hug.

"I'm doin' fine, Angie." What a rotten lie! Here in the Landing I'd often felt like Napoleon jailed out on his rock in the South Atlantic. St. Helena, I think.

She stood back, smiling, eyes aglitter. "No, tell me, really. You look okay. Better'n you did when I left."

At least that was a compliment. I remembered having a terrible cold when she'd flown off the previous year. "I'm down to eight brain cells and two don't work," I confessed.

Then I laughed so she'd know I wasn't totally serious.

"Did you miss me?"

I would have bet every closed gold mine in British Columbia that she'd ask me that. What could I say? "Yeah."

But I didn't put any emphasis on it.

"Why didn't you write to me?"

I'd written her a dozen times and then thrown all the letters away. What was I to say to her—I dream of you every night, I want your kisses, as that song said, I want to hold you, I love you, my lovely Angela? Me, James W. Tidd, saying all that stuff? At age fourteen?

"Jamie, I should have written you, but you don't know how busy I was."

I could imagine.

"Why didn't you write *me*?" she asked again.

I said, "You don't know how busy I was."

She grinned and said, "Ha," and went on up to her house with her mama and papa. I watched her, thinking she might turn around and take another look at me. Wave. Do something.

Angela Ione Pinheiro was a few months past fifteen that summer and her body was already twisting me around. I had to recognize that she'd grown up to be at least a three-quarter woman while in Prince Rupert during the winter rains. Just like that. It was scary. Not only the way she talked, using her hands, tossing her head, but the way she walked. I guess it had really started the last summer when she began taking a full bath every day, no matter how pooped she was coming off Cristo's boat. She had also started wearing some kind of good-smelling perfume even when she went out fishing. It had trailed behind her like a bunch of aerial flowers when she walked down to the float, swinging her fanny in tight jeans.

A photographer from a magazine in Vancouver had come up to take some pictures around our "fish camp" at the Landing. He'd photographed Angie at work, all decked out in her yellow Helly-Hansens, boots on, then cleaning fish with her yellow rubber apron on, a photo of her at the wheel of the boat.

I watched it all going on, thinking that maybe the photographer would ask me to pose too. *Angie's boyfriend helping her hose-down.* He didn't. Neither did she suggest it.

Her head got as big as a watermelon after that magazine came out. But in time all the hot air departed and she acted normal again, not the "Beautiful Fourteen-Year-Old Fisherlady," as the magazine had said.

Angie's long hair was black and shiny, and I didn't see too many flaws in her skin. She had full lips I wouldn't have minded kissing now and then, and a face that probably caused some heads to turn in the high school halls up north. There was usually some mischief in her brown eyes. Without doubt she'd picked up a boyfriend or two during the winter. Without knowing them, I hoped they'd get ruptures during the summer.

Now that she'd come back, what was causing some of my discomfort was that she'd grown regular breasts, not just little knobs, during the winter. In fact, last summer she'd caught me staring at her chest and had laughed. "Wait'll you see 'em next year."

I'd turned my head so fast that I almost snapped

my neck. Very simply, I did not know how to cope very well with this fisherlady Angela Ione Pinheiro.

And she had fulfilled her promise. That was evident. What was between her navel and her chin was now more than adequate.

Papa often called her "that crazy Portogee girl," admiring her for what she could do on Cristo's boat. She could handle nets or haul in a fifty-pound chinook as well as old Cristo. Angie, last of four daughters, all the rest married and gone, could gut and skin a big halibut in thirty seconds. She could also handle old Cristo's number one boat, the *Funchal*, like she'd spin a coin.

But he'd had a problem with her the last year. She was all the time plugged into her Panasonic, bopping all around the deck, and Cristo had to nudge or kick her to communicate. Once he got so mad that he threw her earphones over the side, but then he bought her another set.

Cap'n Cristovão Pinheiro, born on the island of Madeira, was another gillnetter-troller, operating two boats out of the Landing. He'd "jumped ship," just walked away from a Lisbon freighter, in Vancouver Harbor when he was seventeen, and the only time he'd ever returned to Madeira was to bring back his bride, Ione, Angie's plump mother. Angie had been crewing for him since she was nine or ten, first down in the Georgia Strait.

I was taller than Angie, but frankly I don't think I looked as old as she did. But that didn't stop white-haired, dark-skinned Cristo from telling me last year that he'd been watching me. He warned, "Don't tooche Angie."

"I won't," I promised, quaking in my boots.

Funny part, I was always in more danger from her than she was from me.

I told Papa about Cristo threatening me and he laughed. "Just don't tooche her. You know what I mean." Yes, I surely did. Old Cristo was one of the best fish-gutters in the sound.

I told Angie about it too. She also laughed. She said, "Papa is positive my other three sisters were virgins when they went to the altar. He's determined I'll be a virgin too."

My face got red.

The Portuguese people are very romantic and not only make jewelry in the shape of hearts but pillows, bread and cakes, even cheese. Angie, who was big into romance, told me all about this. She once told me a story about a Portuguese nun whose name was Mariana Alcoforado. She was in love with a handsome French officer and wrote him a bunch of letters from the convent in which she was doomed to die. Angie said she wept every time she read those letters.

The Portuguese people are also big on nuns. They even have a dessert called *barrigas de freiras,* or "nuns' tummies," which Mrs. Pinheiro made now and then. I did not go into Angie's house too much when Cristo was around, unless he was asleep, but there were a lot of religious carvings on the walls. One was a big statue under which was "Mary of the Purification." Mrs. Pinheiro always crossed herself when the *Funchal* went to sea, for which I didn't blame her.

Yet despite all the romance and religion, Angie had a side to her that I now recognize as a little bit morbid. She taught me to sing a ditty:

> *El sorte do marinheiro—*
> *E uma verdade pura—*
> *Anda sempre a trabalhar*
> *Em cima da sepultura.*

That translated to:

> The fisherman's fate—
> And this is the truth—
> Is always to work
> Just above his tomb.

At first I didn't get it. Then I realized she was telling me I'd die at sea. She'd come near to being prophetic.

I couldn't wait to tell her about that day in January, the giant wave swallowing the *Dawn Girl* for a moment.

5

*D*awn Girl wasn't going fishing that day—the engine had been running a little rough and Papa wanted to do some fine-tuning—so I hung around the house, thinking that sooner or later she'd come over.

She did, about two o'clock, and after talking with Mama for a few minutes about Prince Rupert, and how glad she was to be back "home" (she said it with a straight virginly face), off we went up Lumber River Trail. There wasn't much choice about going other places. Either stay at the house or go to the old cannery or down to the boats or up the trail. The latter offered privacy, at least.

That trail, hugging along the riverbank, was first used by the Indians when they had some villages in the interior. It was really very pretty walking up that path in spring and summer when the sun leaked through. There was occasional salal and salmonberry and black twinberry mixed in with mostly spruce. Moss-covered trees had fallen here and there across the trail and were rotting away. The spongy, damp earth was covered with moss, and more hung from the branches, dripping most of the time.

I said, "You had some nerve telling Mama you were glad to get back here. She knows better."

Angie just laughed. "For the first few weeks it's not too bad."

It was good to have her home. There she was, in those tight jeans, just ahead of me, letting perfume drift back. That day I was sure glad that the only other person my age at the Landing was female.

The river was high, swift, and cold, playing musical rocks as it slid toward the sea. The late spring and summer snow runoff had begun from the mountains behind us. They were festooned with waterfalls. If there was a good time on the B.C. coast, it was now.

Wanting to tell her everything that had happened during the winter, of any remarkable account, I started at the beginning. "We were almost killed in January."

She stopped and looked back, frowning. "How?"

"How else? Got caught out there in seas twenty-five feet high. Never been so scared in my life. Even Papa was scared."

"Where were you?"

"Out by the South Pointers."

She knew the Pointers. They were rocks off Surf Island, with generally thirty to forty fathoms around them. Plenty of water.

"A gale was coming, but Papa thought we could hang around until early afternoon, get a few more fish in the hold, then run for it. You know him. He'll fish right up to the last minute."

"Not worth it, ever. My pa gets a storm warning, in we come."

Old Cristo was wiser than my papa, I expect, and certainly not as hungry.

We started up the narrow slippery trail again and I described the storm, feeling the fear again.

Angie said, "You were lucky."

"Yeah, we were. It was dark when we got up to the float and there was Mama, waiting for us. In the work light, I could see her face. It looked like someone had drained all the blood out. She looked like a walking corpse. You know what had happened?"

Angie shook her head.

"Well, she'd been monitoring Tito Debar's radio and heard that boat north of us calling for help. Tito had stayed in port that day. She started listening after that captain had given his name, so she didn't know who he was. But that skipper sounded an awful lot like Papa and she was sure she'd lost another husband and now a son. She just collapsed on the float as we were tying up, exhaust smoke swirling around her. Papa had to carry her up to the house through the sleet."

We went for another quarter mile up the trail and then used our smarts and turned around. Ahead was a big mother bear and two cubs, not at all unusual for that path by the river. In addition to winter gales in the North Pacific, mother bears were to be avoided.

6

"Just as long as I can get away from here in the winter, I almost don't mind the summer," Angie said.

Well, that was no big surprise. Who would?

After the trail walk, we were sitting on the broken-down loading dock of the cannery, boards missing like snaggle teeth, a platform that hadn't been used since the early 1950s when B.C. Packers closed out operations. But the stink of salmon canning still lingered in the wood. Rusty machinery and vats were still inside the long, narrow shingled building. Boat captains for twenty miles around used the loft for net storage. At least thirty boxes of gillnets were up there.

The day had turned gray and overcast, and the islands across the way, Hecate and Nalau, were sharp, dark lumps on the horizon. Traffic was heavy out in the channel. The *Queen of the North*, out of Port Hardy, had just passed by. The tourist season to Alaska had begun and the big ships paraded north-ward. At night they looked like moving cities.

I said, "It was awful. I like to went out of my mind. Except for a few times, I was even glad to go out on the boat. After you left, I'd go for three or four days without talking to anyone except my folks. How'd you like that?"

"I don't think I could stand it," she said.

The Pinheiros had been at the Landing for three years and could afford to send Angie to Rupert because she stayed with a relative. Cristo was also successful enough to send her. They took a float plane and went up to see her for two weeks at Christmas and had a good time. Just the opposite, Papa and I went after rockfish the day after Christmas, cold enough to freeze cod fins.

I said, "I'd just walk around in circles some days Or I'd go back in the woods and just sit, waiting for a bear to eat me. Along about February, the worst month of all, I thought about stowing away on the *Nootka*. Just jumping on board and hiding somewhere, then getting off at Namu or Bella Bella, or going on up to Rupert to see you at that uncle's house. How about that? Me seeing you in Rupert . . . ?"

She said, "Well, I don't—"

I interrupted her swiftly so she couldn't finish. I didn't want to hear what she was going to say. "I got so I was wishing I could sleep all day and all night. I even thought about committing suicide." I didn't really. "You don't know how bad it can be."

She said, "Listen, on second thought, I don't think the summer is all that good, either. If I wasn't so tired when we get back, I'd walk in circles too."

"I'll tell you one thing, Angie, I'm going to regular school next year whether it's in Rupert or Port Hardy. I hope it's Rupert, so I can see you. Sitting here doing correspondence courses, you can get so mad you want to stuff them into the stove. I did that one day. Put a whole history lesson in the stove."

She laughed.

I looked her straight in the eyes, keeping my vision above her neck. "You have fun up there?"

She nodded, laying on a big, fat satisfied smile. "I met a fantastic boy."

I really didn't want to hear about him. He was trash fish already. Those fish are inedible or not worth skinning.

"His daddy came in to run the big government grain elevator. From Edmonton."

"Same age as you?" I asked.

"Year older. I wanted him to come down here and live in one of the cottages and work on the boats, but his daddy wouldn't let him."

His daddy was right. We didn't need that boy around here.

She broke into a grin. "I can't wait to get my hands on him in September. He is gorgeous. I try to dream about him every night." She laughed and clapped her hands, big eyes shining like brown headlights.

It was when womanly Angie Pinheiro said things like that that I felt like I was a squirt again. For a while the last summer we'd have long, serious talks after the boats came in and I almost felt like we were equals. And the last August twilight last year when she'd kissed me for the first time—on the forehead, not the lips—I had, in fact, fallen in love with her. At the age of thirteen. It was probably the best thing I ever did at Lumber Landing.

That twilight, as we departed, she'd said to me, *"Boa noite, meu amor."*

I did not know that it meant "Good night, my love" until the next day. Had I known the night before, I might have died happily in my sleep.

"What else did you do up there, aside from that boy?" I asked.

Her eyes narrowed as she looked up and down the rickety platform, then over toward her own house, about two hundred feet away. "You won't tell anyone?" *Anyone* meant my own folks. I wasn't about to tell old Cristo anything. I wouldn't have told him if his roof was on fire, if the *Funchal* was sinking.

"Never," I said.

"Well, we had this slumber party in an apartment four stories up, and everybody was daring everybody else to do things. And the girl who lived there—her parents lived there—said she'd give anybody five dollars to walk around her ledge stark naked. Her bedroom was on the corner of that building and the ledge was about a foot wide. Well, five dollars is a lot of money to me and I stripped down and went out on the ledge. Put my butt up against the wall and went around the building, not looking down once."

"You did that?" I asked, getting a mental picture of Angie with her arms spread wide, feet sliding sideways. "Four stories up?" Angie stark naked!

"No sooner than I got into the other window than we heard police sirens and looked down. All kinds of police cars were down there. A fire truck pulled up, then an ambulance. . . ."

My mouth hung open, but I closed it long enough to ask, "Someone see you?"

"Sure, someone saw me, and about five minutes later there was a loud knocking on the door. By that time all of us, six or seven of us, all in nightgowns or pajamas, were watching *How the West Was Won*. The girl who lived in the apartment said to the officer, 'Somebody must be dreaming. There's been no naked girl out on that ledge.' Then we laughed all night about it. Easiest five dollars I ever made."

I shook my head in amazement and said, "Oh, I got to go to Rupert this fall."

Angie said, "Well, I wouldn't have done it if there'd been ice on that ledge."

I thought about that for a moment and then said, "I guess not," the mental picture changing to Angie slipping off and falling four stories, landing in snow, stark naked.

Angie usually left me with all kinds of disturbed feelings every time I talked to her, and this time was certainly no different. One feeling that always bobbed up was that I'd like to add two years to my life and go past her. But Mama had already told me that "no man ever catches up to a woman in the way you're talking about. An' especially to that Portogee girl."

"What else happened in Rupert?" I asked.

Comparing my awful winter in the Landing to what she was doing was maddening. Off and on, mostly on, I'd thought about her all winter. Sometimes at the table when I was supposed to be doing lessons, I'd printed *J* and *A* in the margins of the courses.

"You know. Movies. Ice skating. Dates. A few dances at school. We went up to Mount Hays twice."

I shook my head. She'd been on another planet. I might as well have been hunting coconuts at the North Pole.

"A lot of fun," she said.

I nodded but didn't want to hear any more. And after hearing about Angie stark naked on the ledge four stories up, there wasn't anything I could say to top it. Then I remembered the killer-whale ad.

"Your papa see that ad about the killer whale?"

"I guess so. There was even a story about it in the Rupert *Pioneer*. Right on the front page."

I said, "That means everybody'll be looking for them."

"I suppose."

That subject quickly exhausted, I said, "Well, I guess I better go on home. See you in a couple of days."

Angie grinned and hopped to the ground. "No doubt about that. *Ate logo*"—see you later.

Though the sun wouldn't set for three hours, Papa was already asleep, behind drawn blinds, when I walked the four hundred feet back to our house. My mother was watching *The Cosby Show* off the satellite. Grandpa Braithwaite was responsible for most things in the cottage that had to do with civilization. The new TV set, powered by battery, and the new TV dish were courtesy of my grandfather. We couldn't have afforded the set, much less the dish. Even so, watching was limited because we had to recharge batteries and that cost fuel.

I watched with her for a while and then went on to bed, unable to get the picture of Angie backing around that ledge out of my mind. Not even a red thread on.

A little later Mama came into the room and asked, "What did you and Angie talk about?" Gossip was so scarce at the Landing that even someone's wart was welcome.

"Oh, school and fishing. You know."

She nodded and bent over and kissed me good night, saying softly, "I love you, Jamie."

I responded in somewhat similar words but I'd always had trouble coming right out and saying "I love you." Mama did it easily. I guess most families can do it easily. Angie could. At that time I felt embarrassed when someone said those words to me. I'd feel I suddenly owed them something. Maybe a part of me.

I thought about that for a while and then picked up *Dirt Rider* to read it again. I'd already read it, cover to cover, seven or eight times and would likely read it ten or fifteen times before the July issue arrived.

On page nine there was a color photo of Rick Johnson, the 250cc National Champion. "Ricky J or Mad Dog Johnson or just R.J." He was on a Yamaha 250cc on a hill, throwing dirt, in white gloves and white pants and white boots with black cat heads on them, white helmet with a blue streak over the crown, Roost-D-Flector over his shoulders and back so that if he took a spill the vented red plastic armor would take the impact. He looked as if he'd just come out of *Star Wars,* and staring at the photo, I twisted my hand as if revving the bike and said, low in my throat, "Vvvvvvvvv, vrrrrrrrrroom . . ." That sounds juvenile, but it's the nearest thing to the real thing.

My gas lamp did not go off until almost midnight, though I was due to go out with Papa in the morning. *Dawn Girl* was rigged for trolling—four tall outrigger poles poking up from her, two of them midships, two forward. We'd be hunting for forty- to sixty-pound chinook salmon tomorrow, dragging the silver-colored spoons, with hooks attached, on steel wire behind the boat. Of course they weren't spoons like you found on a table. Just shaped that way, without the handles but with holes drilled in them to receive the hooks. Fish strike at flashing things, thinking they are other fish.

Cristovão Pinheiro and Angie would also head out in the morning in the *Funchal* for the opening of the chinook season and perhaps fish the same area, although Cristo was often very secretive about where he was going. Even Angie was that way.

7

Stained, dirty, chewed up from constant running, gear frayed, and sometimes holding together with rusty wire, the best thing about *Dawn Girl* was the engine that drummed away inside her. The six-cylinder diesel was eighty percent owned by the Bank of Vancouver and was worth more than the boat, though no one dared tell Papa that. Of course our new green monofilament nets, stored up in the cannery loft, were also owned by the bank, maybe fifty percent. Papa was deep in debt.

With a stubby bow, *Dawn Girl* had a single mast and work boom growing out of her cabin section a little forward of midships. Pilothouse perched over a single messy bunk where I often slept, there was also a grease-spattered cubbyhole galley and storage space. On her cluttered afterdeck were bins for the nets and a power-driven drum to haul them in. Though we could hand-line for bottom fish or troll, as we'd just done, Papa used her exclusively as a gillnetter during the salmon money season of late summer and autumn.

Though my muscles ached and my eyes stung from

lack of sleep, I was almost enjoying myself. I could look at the wake of the boat and see that I was steering a nearly straight course on the flat surface. As Papa had recently told Mama, I was already a fine boat handler.

With about eight hundred dollars' worth of big king salmon in the hold, we were sliding across the millpond waters of Fitz Hugh Sound toward the buy barge, the barge where we'd sell our fish, then drive homeward. Trolled fish are the best-looking species of all because they have no net marks and are usually sold for immediate eating.

Suddenly, far ahead, I saw the vapor of a whale spout. The sun was still high and wouldn't set until almost ten, causing patches of glare where it wasn't hidden by lazy, broken clouds. The sky was ivory-colored. But the puff remained for a few seconds to the right of the glare patches. I wondered what it was. Minke whale? Humpback? Straggler gray headed for Alaska? All three came up inside the sheltered water for one purpose or another.

Perched on his high stool nearby, Papa was saying, "What most people don't realize is that salmon go home to spawn by smell. Memorize the smell of their own stream an' go to it like it was marked on a map. Isn't that somethin', Jamie, fish bein' able to smell an' go back where they were born by sniffin'?"

I didn't even bother to acknowledge that bit of fact, having heard it so often. Though he was only thirty-nine, Papa repeated himself a lot, like an old man. In addition to that habit of repeating himself, Papa was always a little groggy going home after fishing. Often rambling on just to stay awake. Sometimes he'd fish for three days without sleep.

I remember how he looked that unforgettable evening—the original Viking, black wool ski cap sheathing his skull, pulled down to the level of his bushy eyebrows. Papa was a big-boned, redheaded tree trunk of a man, with heavy, hairy forearms and thick shoulders, muscles created from handling nets by hand as well as by power drums. He'd grown up on gillnetters, purse seiners, and trollers, the way his own daddy had grown up. He'd fished from Washington's Cape Flattery clear to the Bering Sea. I wasn't at all sure he wanted me to do the same thing. We didn't discuss it.

But I personally wanted no part of this life, though I didn't tell him that. I thought I'd like to live in the desert, where they have sunshine four hundred days a year.

Papa went on as we motored steadily toward the buy barge, "More'n a thousand streams an' rivers for 'em to find an' they do it somehow. That's a miracle, Jamie."

Barely listening but always sensing I should say something so he wouldn't think I was asleep, I murmured, "Um-huh," and again squinted into the glare, trying to pick up another spout. I'd long ago learned to take advantage of whatever shows nature provided. Sometimes I'd sit for an hour at the kitchen window, using the binoculars to scan the boat traffic or look over to Hecate Island, about four miles off, or south down to Calvert.

"Gets in your blood, all right, them sockeye runs," Papa continued on his broken record. "You know, Jamie, my own daddy, after makin' these runs for forty years, got tears in his eyes when he couldn't go out due to arthritis. He'd watch me go through the break-water an' get all blubbery."

I nodded just to be polite, still searching the waters ahead for that whale.

"Now, it may be that you have to be born into this life, like you and me. I saw my daddy get old before his time. His hands always sore an' puffed."

I remembered. Grandpa Tidd's hands looked like big knotted turnips.

"Hurt muscles keepin' him awake at night."

I glanced at my own right hand. A forty-pound chinook had chomped down on it, sharp teeth projecting from that lower jaw. Sore hands went with the business, everybody knew. My left one was doing the steering. Well, I had no intention of getting old before my age. I planned to be "Mad Dog Tidd" on a dirt bike, not a blubbery old man crying when a boat went out past the breakwater. I planned to win money on hot hills.

"Jamie, I got to admit there are some awful days out here, like that storm we got into in January. . . ."

I didn't need to be reminded. People who fished for a living had mud between their ears, as Mama said now and then.

"Cold an' wet, soaked to the skin, an' you get nets ripped on the rocks, an' come home with not enough fish to pay for the fuel. You swear you'll sell the boat, like your mama wants me to do. But you don't do it. You sit aroun' the house for a few days an' then you can't wait to start the engine an' slip the lines. . . ."

The whale spouted again, much closer.

Papa saw it this time. He said, "Hey, look, we're comin' up on an old humptyback."

I said quietly, "I know," feeling satisfaction that I'd spotted it first.

Humpbacks, or "humpies," or, as Papa called them, "humpties," dearly love to come squirting out of flat bay and sound waters near an anchored rowboat, shocking anyone daydreaming over a pole. They slam to the surface with the force of a fifty-ton tank, sheeting out spray, echoing the splat back through the lines of evergreens ashore. They do it for sheer joy.

I swear humpties can bring their big bodies out of the water a good ten feet and do a complete barrel roll before splashdown. In addition to being good gymnasts, humpties are also fine singers. They fill the ocean chambers with grand opera, according to Papa.

Just looking at a humpty made me laugh. They are natural clowns, with a pleated lower lip, a stubby dorsal fin, and long white flippers. The body is mostly gray-black, with a dark belly. They have knobs and bumps, great warts, all over their heads and flippers, which are also populated with barnacles and parasites. They'd often come up into Fitz Hugh Sound just to scrape the pesky barnacles and parasites off.

I said, "There's something else up there."

Papa took the binoculars, made a quick adjustment for his eyes, and muttered, "Blackfish . . ."

"That's what I thought," I said. Killer whales had come into Fitz Hugh once again.

Papa said, "Whew, we may be in for a show." He took over and moved the wheel slightly to head *Dawn Girl* to the spot where the humptyback was last seen. "That humpty is surely in for a bad time."

I agreed. I'd seen this "show" twice before and it wasn't very pretty. The first time a big killer was playing with a seal before eating it. He was tossing it up into the air like a gray ball. Then the killer opened his mouth wide and the seal just disappeared. The second time I'd seen two blackfish go after a minke whale. I almost vomited before that was over.

Three dorsal fins, two small ones and a huge one, were now slicing through the smooth water. Shining black triangles. I'd heard that those fins were completely boneless, about as thin as a dog's ear at the tip. The black triangles had begun to circle the spot where the humpty had last blown.

Papa said, "Keep your eyes on the big one," and slowed the Volvo to an idling purr as we got closer. Then he disengaged the screw and we drifted.

Less than a minute passed before we were about two hundred feet away from the fins. The killers paid no attention to us. The circling continued, relentlessly.

I saw Papa picking up the Nikon that Grandpa Braithwaite had given Mama two Christmases ago. She always made sure Papa took it along, but he'd used it only three or four times, photographing big or unusual fish. He was focusing just as the humpback broke water.

The camera clicked.

Even before the stream of moisture could shoot up from the humpty's blowhole, the two smaller blackfish were at his lower lip, hanging on. Then the big one leapt into the tan sky, a black and white tube of muscle, thudding his tons squarely on the back of the humpty.

The camera clicked.

"You see that, Jamie?" Papa yelled. "You may never see it again. I hope to God I got it. That killer is a monster. He may be six or seven tons. You see the size of him? Biggest one I ever seen."

Yes, I saw him. He *was* a monster. I felt my heart pounding.

When that humpty came out of the water, like a submarine surfacing straight up, these two smaller blackfish were locked on his lip and he pulled them clear of the water. It was the most horrible thing I'd ever seen. The time before when I'd watched killers attack a humpty they'd gone after his flukes, not his mouth.

Papa said, "We can't hear it but you know what's goin' on down there? Howlin' an' screechin'. These things can talk to each other below the surface."

With the blackfish still clinging on, the humpty rose out of the water again, in panic. Red froth had begun to streak the alabaster patches of the killers.

Even Papa, who'd seen just about everything there was to see out on the water, was amazed by this show. He said, "I've seen starving wolves attack a caribou, but they're nice and gentle compared to what these fish are doin'."

He kept triggering the Nikon, thinking that Mama would never believe what was happening unless she saw the photos.

I said, "Can't he fight back?" I felt sorry for that humpty to the point of stomach sickness.

"Not a chance," Papa murmured. Then he said, "Look!"

The big killer cleared the surface again and crashed on the humpback up near its skull as the strong flukes of the smaller ones drove downward, pushing their victim up, preventing him from diving. The humpback was helpless.

Blood was mixing into the water just below the churned surface as the humpty attempted to roll on his side and fling the groupies from his lips. His flukes flailed, breeching the surface, but the little killers rolled with him, hanging on.

The big one leapt again, at least fifteen feet into the air, slamming down with the force of wet sandbags, sheeting spray.

I never thought I'd ever cry over any stupid fish, but I felt tears in my eyes.

Stunned, unable to breathe, the humpback soon began to drift. The movements of his flukes weakened. We watched as he tried to gather strength for one last effort, but again the tons landed on his skull, the way a wrestler slams down. Bleeding heavily, the humpback surrendered his fifty feet to the killer whales.

In awe, Papa said, "I never watched anythin' like that. What about him leapin' up? Whew!" He kicked the gear in, opened the throttle, and the *Dawn Girl's* screw whirled.

I went to the stern, looking back at the drifting hulk of the opera-singing whale, sharp spikes of dorsal fins around it. Red streaks were in the water for several hundred yards. My heart was still pounding, and now that it was over, I felt a great sadness.

Returning to the pilothouse to stand beside Papa, I said, "Wish we could have helped him." There was a high-powered rifle strapped up in the cabin. Though it might not have done more than sting them, Papa had shot at sharks several times.

Papa said, "Nothin' less than a gunboat could have helped him. Say, I was jus' standin' here thinking 'boot that ad we saw. Remember? A hundred thousand, U.S., for a big blackfish. Well, I'll tell you that the one we just saw qualified. I bet he's close to thirty feet."

Thinking of him smashing the skull of that fifty-foot humpty, I said, "I'd hate to be the one to try an' catch him."

Papa laughed. "I'd hate to be underneath him if he jumped. He'd make splinters out o' this boat."

Well after chalky dark, when the Kelpie Point light was warmly flashing out, the killers were feeding luxuriously, I'm sure. From what I know now, the humpty's tongue, always a delicacy, went first. Torn out by the roots. I'm sure the humpty was still alive when they took it but died shortly thereafter from loss of blood.

By dawn, which was around 4 A.M., the trio was likely satisfied and the remains of the humpty were left to Pacific dogfish, salmon shark, and sixgill cow shark. Even crabs would have a meal in time. The tiny pieces of red flesh that were torn loose during the ripping of the interlocking teeth were probably shared by fingerlings and lucky gulls that had gathered when all the commotion began.

From what I know now, the trio went north, having killed, bellies full, loping away from the gruesome scene like Old West badmen.

8

"You wouldn't have believed it," I said to Angie, after describing what those blackfish did to that poor humpback.

She said, "Yes, I would. They don't have those teeth to grind up herring. Bite-size to them is like a fifty-pound halibut slab four feet long."

We were sitting on the after rail of the *Funchal*. I'd seen her walk down to the boat and had followed her. She'd put some paperbacks on board to read going to and coming from the fishing grounds. The *Funchal* had an automatic pilot, so no one needed to be on the wheel a lot of the time. She read adult romances.

I said, "You realize how big that humpty was?"

She said, "Makes no difference to a black. They'd go after Moby Dick."

"How do you know how big Moby Dick was?"

"I saw the movie. He was the size of a moving van."

Looking back, one of the things that always bothered me about Angie—and there were a number of things that did—was that she always acted like an expert and tried to put me down. She could not let me have the satisfaction of knowing more than she did. Or it seemed that way.

If I said "I heard about that new video sounder, shows you everything under the boat in eight colors . . ." she might answer, "Yeah, that's the one with microprocessor control. . . ."

I'd just stand there and quiver.

Or I might say, to get away from boats and fishing, "Did you know that a tiger's stripes are on his skin as well as on his coat?" She'd answer "Just like a leopard's spots. Shave a leopard and there they are."

I told Papa about getting topped every time by her and he said there was nothing worse in a woman, he'd never recommend marrying her. Mama overheard it and said, "I doubt she'd have either one of you."

I'd even written to Grandpa Braithwaite asking him to give me a book of unusual facts for next Christmas.

"Well, Angie," I said, "what happened out there today is something I never want to see again."

"Chances are you won't," she said as if she was certain.

And upon what was she basing that statement?

We walked on up toward the cottages. It was after nine and still light enough to read small print outdoors but most of the adults were either asleep or watching TV. During fishing season most of the skippers were asleep by eight-thirty. Papa, for one. Always.

Angie opened her door and looked into the living room, then said, "Come on in."

Old Cristo was safely in bed and so was her mother, lucky for me. This many years later I still can't figure out why they didn't trust me. Here I was right under their noses, innocent as first October snow. What did they think was going on up in Prince Rupert during the winter? Necking so heavy that the furnaces could be turned off. Out-of-sight, out-of-mind was what they were doing with Angie. And I had to suffer.

There were two movies on that night, one a Frank Sinatra and Raquel Welch detective thing, *Lady in Cement*, and the other one, *Murphy's Romance*, with Sally Field and James Garner. Well, there was no question as to what Angie would watch. Romance, hot and heavy or just routine. She liked both.

It had already started when we sat down on the couch. It didn't bother her that I left only about a half inch between my hip and hers. In fact, once she started watching, I'm not even sure she knew I was there. Angie always got so involved in movies that she might as well have gotten into the tube with the actors. I think someone could have moved out all the furniture, except the couch and TV, without her noticing it.

I went even closer to her, put an arm around her shoulder, and dropped my other hand casually to her knee while James Garner and Sally Field were dancing at a Western hoedown.

Suddenly old Cristo was there, in his longies, blocking out Garner and Sally, yelling at me to get my dirty hands off Angie. Dirty?

I guess he'd gotten up to go to the bathroom and saw us in there, me about as close as clamshell lips and just as harmless. I came off the couch in a leap, saying, "Cap'n Pinheiro, all I was doing was watching a movie." I'd had an unsettling dream about him the winter past. He was waving a fire ax at me.

Mrs. Pinheiro had come out in her yellow night-gown and was talking in Portuguese.

Angie had gotten up, too, and was saying, "Daddy, please go back to bed."

"*Fora! Fora! Fora!*" he was yelling at me—Out! Out! Out!—and that's exactly where I went, shaking my head.

Angie came out behind me, gave me one of those mild cheek kisses, and said, "I'm sorry."

9

*T*wo days later, dense early summer fog, never a stranger to these waters, came marching across the outer islands in a wall a hundred feet high, both shorelines of Fitz Hugh vanishing in seconds. Angie cut the Evinrude and we began to drift in the Pinheiros' sixteen-foot fiberglass skiff.

We were returning from Critchelow village, north of us, with twenty gallons of white gas for the house lamps plus some groceries for both families. Mrs. Pinheiro was out of olive oil, catsup, and toothpaste; my mother needed baking powder, ammonia, and some other things. All of the families at the Landing usually shopped in bulk, but now and then we'd all need items of one kind or another.

Angie was at the stern running the outboard and I was up on the bow as lookout, which was more important than steering. While most driftwood pieces were small, every so often there'd be a log floating just beneath the surface. Logs do not like boats and vice versa.

Sensibly, I said, "Angie, why don't we head into shore and tie up until it lifts?" No big deal. The current was setting north and soon we'd drift back to Critchelow, where we'd bought the supplies.

There was no sense in groping around in the wet thickness. And without the engine noise, boat noises from the middle of the sound and the muffled caws and croaks of ravens onshore could be heard. Just head for the talkative ravens and we'd bump up on-shore. The water is so deep in Fitz Hugh, sometimes twelve hundred feet, mostly deep right to the shore-lines, that there is no channel as such. Ships and big boats cut a course down the middle. But only ships and boats with radar could navigate in this murk, and even then they slowed way down. They could be heard out in the middle, mournfully blowing foghorns.

We were about a half mile offshore, I estimated, but there was no danger. I'd been in plenty of thick soups in the sound. You either sit and wipe water off your face or putter on into shore. Out in the ocean, it is different, of course. You lay a compass course back to the coast, and pray.

"It'll lift in a minute," Angie said.

"Since when are you an expert on fog?" Sometimes it hung around for a week.

When it was misty, B.C. waters sometimes got a little spooky. All along the shores were ghost villages and beached boats rotting away, some charred. There were deserted shacks that had belonged to miners or trappers or mink farmers and abandoned fish camps. There were sacred Haida or Coast Salish or Kwakiutl burial and ceremonial grounds. There were little is-lands that people said were haunted. Quite a ways from us, all the trees on Sorrow Island were gnarled or stunted.

The mist was so thick that I could see her only as a vague form at the stern, though I wasn't fifteen feet from her. But there'd been times at the Landing when I couldn't see the cannery building ten feet away. B.C. coast has some championship fogs.

Suddenly we heard killer-whale talk out there, and thinking of what I'd seen the other day, I felt a ticking in my stomach. Sticking their heads out of the water, blackfish talk to each other in whistles, clicks, buzzes, screams, and snorts. They make a lot of different sounds, the ones above water seeming to come from the blowhole region, not the mouth. Killer whales are well known for their piercing screams. Any scream in a dense fog, human or blackfish, is apt to tighten your windpipe.

I'd often heard them talking when they came up and fooled around off Lumber Landing. I'd also heard them talk before in the fog. Where were they? What did they have on their spooky minds? It was eerie—foghorns blowing, faint caws of the ravens, now killer-whale talk.

I said, "Angie, you hear that?"

The boat was still drifting northward, water slapping at it. "Sure I heard it. Just some blackfish gossip."

"They may be the ones we saw yesterday. I wouldn't want to tangle with them," I said, putting myself into the position of yellow chicken without thinking she'd take advantage. But I was speaking the truth.

In fog, even when blackfish aren't around, the splashing and thrashing of big fish nearby gets to you. A gray whale once spouted not ten feet from us in dense fog and even Papa jumped when we heard that whoosh.

"They don't usually eat people," Angie said. "I read about them a long time ago in *Reader's Digest*. They make a mistake now and then, but not often."

I could see only this dark smudge in the stern that was Angie Pinheiro. I bit. "What kind of mistake?"

"Well, I remember something about a blackfish being under the ice at the South Pole and seeing a shadow up on top. The whale thinks it's a seal and comes out from under the ice, skids across, and bites this man half in two before he realizes it isn't a seal."

I said, "Thanks a lot, Angie."

"And there was another case in the same story about some blackfish eating the bottom out of a sailboat near the Galápagos. But maybe they don't like fiberglass."

Great, I thought. Angie had done this kind of thing to me before.

Meanwhile, the killer whales, whichever blackfish they were, were clicking and whistling not more than a hundred yards from us, continuing to make me nervous. I had no desire at all to see the big one again.

I said, "Angie, start that engine and let's go over to shore and tie up."

With a certain cunning in her voice, she asked, "Jamie, you afraid?"

"Not as long as I'm in this boat." You bet I was afraid of a twenty-five-foot blackfish!

Then that insane Portogee girl, about whom I'd always had a lot of mixed feelings, began to singsong, "Who's afraid of a killer whale, a killer whale, a killer whale?" I still couldn't see her very well. She remained a shape that was acting like a six-year-old.

I yelled at her to shut up.

She kept going for a couple more verses, mocking the big, bad wolf, then laughed long and hard. I was ready to crawl back and bash her one, but that wasn't such a good idea, either. Angie Pinheiro would hit back with a closed fist as hard as she could.

Then there was a tremendous splash not a hundred feet away and Angie gasped, "What was that?"

I knew what it was and my stomach came up around my teeth. The big black slamming down, the way he'd done on that humpty. Another leap and he could be in our laps.

Angie had shut her mouth.

It got quiet again out there and I noticed that even the blackfish had stopped yapping. Whether that was good or bad remained to be seen.

I said, "Angie, let's go ashore and tie up."

"All right," she said, sounding a little subdued. The Evinrude fired off.

There was no danger of us getting lost if we steered toward the raven croaks. They were land-bound and acted as beacons.

We motored toward shore for about ten minutes and then she cut the noisy engine, and as the sound died away I knew we were only a hundred feet from land. In addition to the raven screeches, we could hear puffins and auklets. And, of course, you can always smell the rain forest.

A jarring thump, and I knew the skiff had grounded. I said, "Okay, let's tie her up and just wait." We swung broadside.

Angie didn't say a word, and I waited another few seconds before saying, "Angie?" Then I scrambled to the stern, realizing she was no longer aboard.

I thought for a moment. She hadn't said anything since she'd cut the motor. But I hadn't heard a splash out there. I was sure she hadn't fallen overboard.

I went forward and grabbed the bow line, jumping ashore. Feeling around with my boots, I finally found a stump and tied off the skiff, yelling for Angie at the same time. "You playing some kind of game with me?"

No answer. Not a single sound from her! Or of her! Feeling a mixture of anger and now a little anxiety— could she have fallen overboard in that deep water?— I stood absolutely still a moment, hoping to hear her move around. She was way too old to be playing hide-and-seek games with anyone. But one never knew exactly what would happen with Angie.

I was guessing we were about four miles below Critchelow, maybe near the remains of the fish camp and cannery at Little Norway. We hadn't been under way for more than twenty minutes when the fog rolled in.

Now that I thought of it, I was absolutely sure she hadn't fallen overboard. Anyone who got into this water at least made a gasp. I'd done it several times, so I knew.

Debating a moment whether or not to stay by the boat or try to find out where she was, I called out again and again, only to be answered by ravens and auklets. Then I started groping inland, a foot at a time, trying to find a landmark.

Because there were some rotting stumps, I knew we were close to Little Norway, but the camp itself was just a bunch of falling-down shacks. Nobody had lived there for years.

Every few feet I'd stop and yell for Angie. I was, in

truth, beginning to think that something bad had happened to her. But I soon learned I was out of my head to waste my sympathy even if she was drowned.

Not two minutes later, after I'd slipped on moss and tumbled into a puddle, the fog pulled back, as it usually does, like a gray curtain yanked up, leaving only drifting wisps. Strong sun flushed out.

And there, ten feet away, was Angela Ione Pinheiro, sitting on the ground, her back against a burial stone, acting dead. We were in that tiny cemetery, maybe twelve graves, just south of Little Norway. Her eyes were closed and her tongue was hanging out, mouth deformed. She looked like she'd just been hung and cut down.

I yelled at her, "Damn you, Angie, get up off there." I was tempted to kick her.

She couldn't hold the deformed look any longer and began laughing.

"Don't you know I have a D.B.?"

"What's a D.B.?" I yelled.

"Diseased brain."

"You certainly do," I said. "Let's go before the fog sets in again."

Then she laughed some more and got up.

I turned on my heel and went back to the skiff, which wasn't more than two hundred feet away.

In a few minutes we headed on back to Lumber Landing, not talking very much.

10

More or less, that's how it'd been from the start. I'd first seen Angie two summers past when the *Funchal* came idling up to the floats, along with Cap'n Pinheiro's other boat, the *Machico*, both loaded with furniture and household supplies. New people, new boats always attracted attention at the landing. New faces were always welcome.

Suddenly this dark-haired, red-cheeked girl in a worn gray parka and blue woolen cap jumped off the *Funchal*, bow line in hand, like she knew what she was doing. She flipped it over a cleat as her papa backed down, jumped nimbly back aboard to grab the stern line, and zapped that around another cleat. She was all business, I could see.

Standing on the float, I said hello.

She nodded and quickly dropped a trio of rubber tire casings along the inboard side to act as fenders. She knew how to crew.

Walking over, I said, "I'm Jamie Tidd, off the *Dawn Girl.*" I wanted to let her know I crewed too.

She told me her name, then disappeared into the wheelhouse and little forward cabin.

Meanwhile, Papa asked Cap'n Pinheiro why he'd come to desolate Lumber Landing. "Too many boats down there," the Portogee said, pointing south.

"Me, too," said Papa, with a laugh. We'd arrived a month earlier, the *Dawn Girl* loaded with what possessions we had. Too many boats operating in the Georgia Strait. During salmon runs, skippers were dodging nets and buoys all over the water, yelling at each other. Hundreds of boats down there near civilization. Living was rough up here but the fishing was better and easier.

Then the *Machico* docked, Mrs. Pinheiro aboard her.

When Angie came out on deck again I asked, "You need any help unloading?"

She eyed me, sizing me up, I now realize, then said, "All we can get," giving me a nice, toothy smile. I think she'd already figured our age difference, me halfway over eleven, Angie pushing thirteen. But it was probably the way I acted, kind of awed by her, not the way I looked.

That afternoon I must have carried twenty-five boxes up to Cottage 7, the one they'd occupy. Every male not at sea pitched in to help the newcomers. Once I saw her struggling with a heavy wooden crate and went up to say, "Here, let me help you." *A mistake!*

"You sure?"

"I'm very strong," I said, wanting to show off. *I might not be as old as you are but I'm stronger.* I'd been crewing, handling fishing gear, getting muscles since I was seven.

Then Angie got behind me, with a smaller box, as I staggered up the slope, legs threatening to cave in,

arms aching. Gritting my teeth, I got within twenty
feet of their doorway before I dropped it, the crate
mashing my toes.

Helping me up, she suggested we both carry it the
rest of the way. I could feel the crimson on my face.

Score the first big one for older, wiser Angie
Pinheiro.

At supper that night Mama said, "That new girl is
sure pretty."

I replied, "Is she?" knowing that she was.

"Something wrong with your eyes, Jamie?" Papa
asked.

I shook my head.

Mama said, "Well, you've got someone to pal
around with this summer."

"I'd rather it had been a boy," I said.

Papa said, "From what I saw of her on that deck,
she's boy enough."

As far back as I could remember I'd been uncomfortable with girls, and I hadn't been around all that
many. Yet I don't know that I was too much different
from other boys, even when I went to regular school
in Vancouver, before we brought the *Dawn Girl*
north. We did boy things. They did girl things.

That first summer I truthfully didn't know what to
talk about aside from fishing and the weather and
dirt bikes. The latter didn't seem to interest her at all.

Toward the end of that first summer I got so I'd
actually hide from her, not knowing what to say. The
second was a little better, and now ten days into this
third one I thought I was almost holding my own
with Angie, despite Little Norway.

11

With the new, lightweight monofilament nets in their bins, ready to trap sockeyes during the night, we went out of the Landing about five-thirty in the afternoon and Papa said to me, "Okay, jus' angle on out toward the middle an' put her on three-forty an' we'll go up off Koeye an' see what's doin' there."

Cristo and Angie had gone out about noon, Cristo refusing to say where he planned to fish, as usual.

Papa got busy checking the floats and lead lines, the red-and-white-colored buoys marked PT, hoping to put the nets into the water by seven o'clock and then let them soak all night, trapping hundreds of salmon in the meshes. Tomorrow was the first day of the four-day sockeye opening.

Busy checking gear, he wasn't prepared for my shout: "Those blackfish are back! Same ones, I think!" Maybe the same ones Angie and I had heard out in the fog?

Papa's head swiveled around, eyes sweeping the water. Cloud cover and mist had turned Fitz Hugh gray and chill.

"Over toward Wilwilli."

Papa scrambled up beside me, grabbing the binoculars. "Yeah," he said, "same ones." His hand pulled back on the throttle, slowing the boat. "That's the same leapin' back-buster, all right." I reminded myself to tell Angie we'd met 'em again.

Wilwilli Cove was at the mouth of Wilwilli Creek, a little hidden crystal stream about a mile north of Lumber Landing. Game often splashed along the swift, cold creek to feed and then emerged from the forest thickness to survey the cove, which was owned mostly by birds. Timber-lined, a north-south, spoon-shaped body of water, it could be entered, at risk, through a narrows about a hundred yards wide and eight feet deep at high tide. A sandbar was usually present at the entrance, and no wise boatman went into Wilwilli unless he had to. Nonetheless, with two massive, guano-spattered rocks on either side of the entrance, the cove, hollowed out by gushing summer runoff from the snow peaks, was a protected bottle.

I'd walked up there a dozen times just to look around, having nothing better to do at the Landing. Sometimes the trail was less than a yard wide. I usually spotted bears inspecting for fish. I let them alone and they did the same to me. It was a pretty cove, about a quarter mile long and half that wide.

I said, "Those other two are still with him, the smaller ones." Same ones that had been talking in the fog.

Easing the wheel to starboard, Papa said quietly, as if he was afraid they'd hear him, "I see 'em."

The smaller ones were separated from the giant back-buster and swimming lazily to the north of the cove.

Papa said tensely, "I wonder if he is goin' to do it?"

"Do what?"

"Get himself trapped!"

Watching the killer intently, Papa was slowly building speed on a course headed straight toward Wilwilli. "Keep your fingers crossed, Jamie. Here comes Maui an' your motorbike, school in Prince Rupert, an' a new boat for me! Good God Almighty, boy, we can get rich. *Rich!*"

In disbelief after what we'd seen on Sunday, I asked, "You're going to try and catch him?"

"You bet!"

"How?"

"Drop a couple of nets across that cove entrance is how. If he goes up in there, an' gives me five minutes, he's a caught blackfish. I don't care how big he is."

The heart-pound that I experienced on Sunday began to return. With it, an overwhelming feeling of excitement mixed in with fear. That whale was truly a killer. He seemed bigger than our boat.

He moseyed on into the cove, swimming leisurely, the great dorsal fin a black sail. They sometimes explore coves if the water is deep enough. Nosing around in them, pinging ahead for food. I'm sure he heard the racket of the *Dawn Girl*, the thrash of our propeller, but he seemed not to pay any attention at all. Fishing boats throbbed and thrashed all over the coastal waters, which were his home.

Papa shoved the throttle full and *Dawn Girl* went for the south entrance rock wide open. Papa said, breathlessly, not like the calm man I knew best, "Jamie, he's in the bottle. Here, take the wheel an' do exactly as I say. Steer for South Rock, come up alongside it, an' I'll tell you when to hit reverse."

He went back to the stern and stood by the big

roller on the transom, grasping one of the net anchors, tying it to the net.

I shouted back, "Can't he bust right through?"

Thinking of the humptyback slaughter, I wasn't at all sure we should try to capture that whale, no matter Maui and a dirt bike. Even a fifty-pound fish could tow a human around like a feather. This blackfish had to weigh five or six tons or more and, as Papa had said, could smash the boat with one leap.

Papa yelled back, "No, no, he won't. Put anything in front of him and he gets confused. The boys up at Namu told me that."

I tried to concentrate on the cove entrance and South Rock, still not believing that any net could hold that big an animal.

Papa didn't believe it, either, he confessed later. But it was worth losing a net just to try it.

As the boat closed on the entrance Papa shouted, "We get him an' we got a hundred thousand. Hear that? He's over twenty-five feet an' in good condition. You saw how he jumped on Sunday."

Sweat began to pop out on my forehead, my heart was pounding. I felt like we were doing something wrong. This wasn't a game fish, an eating fish. This was a mammal.

Papa shouted, "Okay, now, Jamie, I want you to lay the starboard side right up against the rock and give me full reverse when I yell."

I turned the *Dawn Girl* in a tight half circle, the boat now running at quarter speed.

Papa shouted, "That's the way!"

Dawn Girl was closing on the rock.

"You're doin' fine, Jamie," Papa yelled.

A thrill now pushed away at the fear. But my mouth was dry.

Papa shouted, "Reverse! Full throttle!"

I slammed reverse in and sent the Volvo wide open. *Dawn Girl* came to a halt, rearing back.

As Papa leapt to the rock to plant one end of the net anchor into a crevice, he shouted, "Stop engine."

Dawn Girl stayed in position long enough for him to jump back on board.

"Okay, straight ahead, half throttle," he yelled, and began paying out the net over the free-spinning iron roller.

I peered into the cove as we began crossing the entrance, green mesh flowing out behind the boat, lead line carrying it to the bottom of the cove and the polyfoam floats pulling it erect. At the north end of the cove I spotted the dorsal and yelled to Papa, "He's still up in there."

He grinned up at me, "Damn right he is." I'd never seen him this excited over anything.

In less than a minute the *Dawn Girl* was a hundred feet away from the dung-whitened North Rock and Papa yelled, "Okay, do the same thing. Give me full-throttle reverse when you get near, then stop her."

I performed to near perfection and Papa jumped again, securing the other anchor in the rock, making a tie on the net so we could double it back. "We got him, Jamie, we got him," he shouted jubilantly, then leapt back aboard.

The blackfish was still deep in the cove, scouting around, though there wasn't usually anything of special interest in it except the taste of fresh water and sediment that had spilled down from the mountains.

The sockeye runs up Wilwilli did not begin until late August.

The net was now stretched from rock to rock, anchored firmly, snug against the bottom. The line of red and white floats bobbing on the surface told us that we'd succeeded. But twice more I made the run between the two big rocks to drop more net. Three layers now trapped the killer inside the cove.

"What more can we do?" I asked as Papa guided the boat back to the center of the cove.

"We drop the hook an' wait. Go on up on the bow an' let her go when I say."

I crawled forward while Papa positioned the boat. Then I knelt by the anchor winch, tripping it when Papa yelled, "Let 'er go."

In a few minutes the *Dawn Girl* rode to the line, stubby bow pointing toward the mountains. I stayed up there and Papa soon joined me, turning off the engine.

Not long after, having satisfied his curiosity, the killer whale decided to depart Wilwilli Cove and rejoin his two companions, who were now about a quarter mile offshore. We could see their smaller dorsals. The black moved slowly and warily toward the nets, huge body about four feet below the surface.

We knelt on the bow, eyes glued to the ripple of water in which was centered the dorsal fin. I thought to myself, Well, he's picking up speed, and I'll have to spend all day tomorrow helping Papa mend the net.

The ripple of water came on, growing into a tiny wavelet, and in a moment we could see his full length.

"Good God," Papa gasped. "He must be forty feet."

Holding on to the snubbed anchor rope, fearing

that the blackfish might attack the boat, as Angie had said happened off the Galápagos, I was swallowing pure fear. I found my tongue to ask, "Can he turn us over?"

"I doubt it," Papa said tensely, unsurely.

The blackfish approached to within three feet of the barrier and seemed puzzled by it, then he turned north, looking for an opening. From the boat, brown eyes, set way back in his head, and the gleaming white skin on his head and beneath his jaws were clearly visible. For a flash we could see his ugly crocodile teeth. There must have been fifty of them, pointing slightly backward and conical in shape. They looked like they could easily take a chunk out of the *Dawn Girl*. But I looked into his eyes fleetingly and they seemed to be without fear or anger. Just puzzlement. No alarm.

Papa began to relax a little as the glistening back undulated slowly toward North Rock. "He's bigger than an elephant," Papa said.

He wiped beads of sweat from his forehead and upper lip, though it wasn't all that hot at Wilwilli that early evening. Then he said, without much conviction, "Those boys at Namu were right. He's buffaloed by a net."

I asked, "Did you see his eyes? He was looking right at us."

"I saw them." Then he laughed. "Don't fall overboard, Jamie."

No way.

The blackfish, snout only a foot from the monofilament, went all the way to North Rock and beyond it, then turned back. He dropped to the bottom and swam not more than a foot above the sand, his flukes raising a cloud. Then he surfaced near South Rock, blowing moisture. Then he made a sound like a creaking door that sent a chill up my spine. There was a whistling answer from the two outside.

"Wish I knew what he's just said!" Papa was staring seaward.

"Me, too." It was beginning to get very nervous out by the center of that net.

The blackfish swept back along the netting, looking up at us again.

I got my first good, close view of him. His throat and belly were alabaster white, and the white circled up, as if painted on, over his sides and back, which was the color of wet charcoal. Another oval of white sat above and just behind his eyes. His round snout was interrupted with those two rows of conical teeth, spaced alternately so they could interlock. An eating machine was what we faced.

Papa said, "Wow," and stood up, making his way around the pilothouse to pick up the CB microphone and call repeatedly for Mama. In a moment she came on. Papa asked cleverly, "Honey, you wanna go to Maui? Over."

Mama answered laughingly, "Why are you calling me to ask that? You just left here. Why didn't you ask me then? Sure, I want to go to Maui."

Papa said, "Well, we jus' got the ticket. Jamie and I trapped that big buster blackfish up here at Wilwilli Cove. Got him right in the bottle."

Mama laughed again. "I don't believe you, Perry Tidd."

"We got him, all right. I swear to it! Jamie, yell to your mother that we got the blackfish."

I did.

"I'll walk right up there," Mama said.

"No, you won't. Look up that ad an' call me back with the number of that guy in Huntington Beach."

I could hear that Mama was still skeptical. "You sure you got that whale, Per?"

"You betcha," said Papa. "Now find that ad."

Mama's voice suddenly took another turn, as might be expected. "Is Jamie all right? Is what you're doing dangerous?"

"We're both fine," said Papa. "We're on the boat an' that fish is behind three layers o' net, an' he's not gonna charge 'em. Don't worry." She would, anyway.

Mama said, "You both be careful. I want to go to Maui but not this bad."

"Get me that number, Lacy. Over," Papa said, and signed off.

Then he got on the radiotelephone to ask any boat with a load of salmon to come by Wilwilli Cove. He said, "I need a half ton an' I'll pay a dime over wholesale. I'll take some ice, too, if you got any to spare."

There went the chinook money we'd made on Sunday. I asked, "How do you know he eats that much?"

"The boys at Namu told me. They were buyin' fish for three weeks. He'll eat three or four hundred pounds a day every other day."

A voice soon crackled back. "You drunk, Perry?"

It was Dick Jahraus on the *Patricia Lou*, another boat that worked out of Lumber Landing.

"Jus' bring me some fish, Dick," said Papa. "I've got a big mouth to feed."

Dick said, "You are drunk, but I'll come by in the morning. Over."

At this moment I don't think the blackfish was aware he'd been captured. It still did not occur to him to gather speed and blast through our net like it was Christmas wrapping.

The killer began to patrol the inside of the net, back and forth, occasionally raising his head to breathe, then buzz and click. By now his companions had moved up closer to the cove entrance, ignoring the boat and us fragile humans. They swam along the net, heads barely a foot from it, as their friend sought a way out. They milled, and blew, and talked to him.

I listened and watched and got more nervous.

A couple of minutes more and the CB came to life with Mama's voice. She read the ad, then said, "I'm coming up there."

Papa picked up the microphone to call B.C. Tel's marine operator in Bella Bella and got patched through to Huntington Beach, California. The Ocean Arena operator had trouble locating Zachary Cooke but finally he was there, saying, "To whom am I speaking?"

"Perry Tidd. I'm a B.C. fisherman."

"You're a what fisherman?"

"British Columbia. Up in Fitz Hugh Sound."

"Oh."

"Mr. Cooke, I got your big killer whale. He's twenty-five feet or more. In good shape."

"You have one? Well, that's great. You're sure he's twenty-five feet?"

"You betcha."

"Where is he?"

"Wilwilli Cove, 'boot a mile north of Lumber Landing."

"Where is that, for God's sakes?"

"In Fitz Hugh Sound. North of Calvert Island."

"How do we get there?"

"Go to Port Hardy at the end of Vancouver Island and charter a helicopter. When will you come up here?"

"Right away. We'll leave in the morning. I'll bring my chief trainer and an expert from Seattle."

"Fine," Papa said. "We'll stay right here. I'll see you soon."

"Hey, don't hang up," Cooke said.

"This call is costing me a fortune," Papa said.

"I'll pay for it," said Cooke. "I want you to understand why we need a big one. Ocean Arena is going to be a huge place, with all kinds of rides and a convention center and hotels. The hotels will have ocean views and we'll give Disneyland a run for its money. The reason we want the biggest killer whale in the world is that we're building the world's biggest killer-whale tank."

Papa looked at me, awed by what had happened so quickly. Convention center? Hotels? Biggest killer-whale tank in the world.

"We're spending millions," said Cooke.

"I understand," said Papa. "I think we've got the biggest blackfish in the world."

"Sensational," said Zachary Cooke. "See you late tomorrow."

"Okay," said Papa, grinning into the mike. "If you need to reach me, my boat is the *Dawn Girl* an' her call number is Charlie Zebra Niner Three Six Four Five. Do you read that?"

"Affirmative," said Cooke.

"Call me through the overseas operator in Oakland."

"Okay," said Cooke.

"Over and out," said Papa.

We took the *Dawn Girl* over to South Rock and tied up.

12

Mama practically ran up that dank trail through the woods to Wilwilli, slipping and sliding. There was feather and hanging moss everywhere, mushrooms and bracket fungus and licorice ferns.

She took one look at the blackfish and said, "That thing scares me to death. Don't either of you fall in there."

We had no intention of doing that. Remembering what Angie had said happened at the South Pole—a killer jumping out to eat a seal and cutting a man in two instead—I stayed three or four feet away from South Rock.

"You know who that man is? That Zachary Cooke? I'll bet he's a former movie star," Mama said.

Papa wasn't a movie watcher.

"And I'll bet that Ocean Arena is owned by a movie studio."

"What do you mean?" Papa asked.

"Well, I read something a while ago about a movie studio buying an unfinished place like Sea World."

Papa laughed. He always said that Mama read the

most useless things. TV and movie gossip columns in magazines that got passed around the Landing.

Mama went on, "He used to be in the movies. Twenty-five years ago. He comes up on the late-lates now."

Papa said, "Whatever he is, I jus' hope he gets here soon. It'll break us jus' to feed this monster. I can't go fishin' now."

I asked, "If he buys it, how will they get it to California?"

Papa said, "Gettin' him to California is their problem. All I want is that check an' we'll pack for Prince Rupert a day later."

Mama said, "Maui," and then kissed Papa and hugged me. "I can't get over it."

We three almost did a dance on the brink of Wilwilli Cove that late twilight. We were all so fired up, it's a wonder we didn't launch off into space.

What kept my feet on the rock was the occasional talking of the whales. I would have given anything to know what they were saying back and forth. *Get the humans?*

Mama soon went on home. She probably floated home that night, heels barely touching the leaf-mold trail. I can't remember when I'd seen her so happy. What I didn't know, and Papa didn't know, was that her silent plans soon would go far beyond Maui.

With the blackfish spouting up at ten- to twenty-second intervals, a wet, whoosing sound that became a little creepy after a while, I didn't sleep much. The other two whales stayed close by the net and bumped the bottom of the boat several times, as if they were testing. Papa, on and off, shone the boat's powerful spotlight around the cove just to make sure our prize wasn't getting ready to make a run for freedom. Once, as if exercising, he made one of those leaps, coming up ten or twelve feet and splashing down.

Papa said, "If he thought about it, he could jump right over the net."

"Why doesn't he?"

Papa shook his head.

Another time, while whistling to the smaller whales, he held his head out of water a long time, eyes glistening in the ivory beam. It reminded me of pictures of the Loch Ness monster, except his head didn't resemble a snake's head and he had no neck. It was more like the end of a huge black and white gun shell, shining in the night.

Sleep was hard to come by since Papa and I were sharing that single bunk. He snored and once rolled over on me. Two hundred and thirty pounds were mashing me until I punched him in the ribs.

Well after daybreak, which came in with a fine drizzle, boats began to stop by to take a look at what was in Wilwilli Cove.

Cap'n Selby said, "He ain't pan-sized, is he, Perry?"

"Not unless you got a pan the size of a roller rink!" Papa said, laughing.

Tito Debar, the youngest captain at the Landing, said, "You finally got lucky, Perry."

"Looks that way." I think Papa was enjoying all the attention.

The skippers joked with him about what he planned to do with all that money. He joked back, saying that Mama had already spent three thousand on airline tickets and hotel rooms in Maui, that I was about to spend a thousand on a dirt bike, and that he'd be lucky to have enough left for a new boat.

Then the skippers went on their way back to the Landing and bed, having already sold good catches to the buy barge at Kwiklit.

About six Dick Jahraus put the *Patricia Lou* alongside the *Dawn Girl* and off-loaded a half ton of salmon plus about five hundred pounds of ice. The fish went into the hold and I shoveled ice over them.

Jahraus, a man as big as Papa and a lot crustier, said, "I'm sure glad I don't have to feed that thing."

"You ought to be," Papa replied. "You gonna give me these on credit?"

"Nope," said Dick. "I only gamble at cards."

Watching him go, Papa said, "Lord, if that man Cooke don't take this blackfish, we're in a heap o' trouble." He'd never missed a sockeye opening since he was a little boy.

Later Mama came out with our breakfast. Cold cod filets and hot biscuits with honey. She'd walked from the Landing. Then about a half hour later my parents went back home on the *Dawn Girl* for a tent and camping equipment, a chain saw for firewood, and to borrow a portable gas generator from Cristo so that the cove could be lit up in the hours of darkness.

Soon some of the wives and small children from the Landing walked up through the woods to take their looks. It was like a side show that we were running at Wilwilli.

Mrs. Selby said, "I think you and your papa are out of your minds. That blackfish is gonna get mad after a while and take that net on out to sea."

"I hope not," I said, explaining that he didn't know the net wasn't solid.

Mrs. Bev Jahraus said, "You just be careful not to fall in, Jamie."

"I'm being careful."

Anette Debar, the youngest wife at the Landing, holding her five-year-old girl tightly by the hand, with another baby already swelling her belly, studied the killer whale for a few minutes, then said, "He's so beautiful he's breathtaking." Then she looked over at me. "Are you sure you want to keep him?"

"We want to sell him, we don't want to keep him."

She started to say something else, but then nodded and told her daughter they had to go.

She didn't approve, I could tell.

The others left, and I was alone again insofar as humans were concerned.

In midmorning, while Zachary Cooke and his people from Ocean Arena were flying toward Vancouver, I sat on South Rock near the net anchor watching the killer whale nose along the monofilament barrier, moving slowly. Confused, I was sure. Once he came swimming right up to me, not five feet from me, one eye surveying. It looked as though he could see sideways as well as ahead. I thought he might be saying, *Why am I here?*

That look that Anette Debar had given me, after asking if we were sure we wanted to keep him, was still on my mind. Bothering me. She was always so gentle.

I remember feeling strange that morning. Not frightened because I was alone there, just strange. The black was obviously puzzled. He had no natural enemies in the sea, none brave enough to take him on. Humans, on land, posed no threat except people like us, I guess. Nor did he appear to connect the barrier now in front of him with the human—me—sitting on the rock staring down at him.

There was still nothing threatening or mean in the eye. No anger at all. I had to look away.

Shaped like a warped marshmallow, South Rock was about eight feet across and twelve long, the color of cinnamon stained by bird dung, an almost flat place to take a sunbath had there been any sun. North Rock didn't look too much different.

I had now been alone with the blackfish and his two companions for almost two hours and I was hoping Papa would soon return with the boat. I knew that I wasn't in any danger up there on the rock, but that chitter-chatter made me uneasy. There was a lot going on. Were they plotting something?

Back in the woods the land birds were chirping and then the sea birds added their cries as the diving loons and kingfishers and cormorants and pigeon guillemots went about finding food. That was all added to the blackfish sounds.

Papa had fed our prize about two hundred pounds of salmon before he took off in the *Dawn Girl*, deciding not to feed the smaller killers, hoping they'd go away. No such luck.

13

*T*oward noon I heard a voice that I knew well and turned around to see Angie coming through the evergreens off the trail to the Landing. The trees were so thick in there that light never penetrated. She was a welcome sight, still wearing her sea boots. The *Funchal* had finally come in after a night of gillnetting.

"Why don't you let that thing loose?" were her first startling words when she got close to me. Typical, but it was something I didn't want to hear. She was watching the blackfish as she walked. There were dried salmon scales on her jeans and faded windbreaker. She wore a beat-up Toronto Blue Jays hat.

"You're kidding," I said, standing up. "Let him go?"

"No, I'm certainly not," said Angie. "Anything that big and beautiful ought to be free to do anything that it wants to do. Anything at all. Let him go!" She was saying what Anette Debar hadn't said.

I said, "Come on, Angie. You know how much this whale is worth?"

"Yeah, I know. And if my papa had caught him I'd tell him the same thing—turn him loose."

By now she'd dropped down beside me, slapping me on the thigh to say hello. "And he'd tell me to get my buns lost. What are you supposed to be doing here? Guarding that thing? Biggest one I ever saw. This the same one that killed that humpty?"

"Yes, and I think it's the same one that splashed down in the fog near us the other day. Now you see how big he is. And maybe you can understand why I was scared."

"He is big," she said, thoughtfully.

"Papa went on back to the Landing with the boat. We're going to set up camp here."

She was prettier than ever this chill, misty morning, I thought. The reds in her cheeks were flaming, and her hair, poking out from around the faded baseball cap, was shiny damp. But she also looked tired, having been up on the *Funchal* all night.

She said, "I saw your papa. He came over to borrow an extra lantern and the ginny. What do you need with electricity up here?"

Before I could answer, she said, "We got a lot of sockeyes last night. Must have been three hundred boats drifting out there. I think this'll be the best season we've had in four years."

"And wouldn't you know we're missing it?"

Then she spotted the pair of blackfish patrolling the nets. "They belong to him?"

"I guess so," I said. "First day we saw him they were with him. And I think they were the ones talking to him in the fog."

"I'll bet they're females," said Angie. "My woman's smarts." She tapped her right temple. "They are named Persephone and Desdemona."

Wondering where she got "Persephone" and "Desdemona," I said, "I don't know what they are, male or female, but I wish they'd go away."

Angie suddenly stood up and shouted to the blackfish, "Hey, big whale, you come here. Right now. Now! This minute!"

I was speechless as the big black, in the middle of the cove, began to swim slowly toward the rock. He came up once to spout, eyes aimed at Angie.

I yelled at her, "Watch out," and got up on my knees.

Angie looked at me scornfully. "What's he going to do? Jump out of the water and get us? This is no ice pack. He's no frog."

Alarmed for both of us, I said, "This whale can jump clear over this rock." Higher, even.

Ignoring me, she moved to the edge and knelt down. "You can train these things like puppy dogs, I've heard. Easier, they say."

Rising, I said, "Come on, Angie, don't get so close to him. This is no tame blackfish. He hasn't been trained. This isn't Sea World."

He swam on up, raising his head out of water, putting his lower jaw on the rock edge, opening the upper one to expose those saw blades. I couldn't believe what I was seeing. He whistled several times through the blowhole.

She said, "You see, he's talking to me." Then making her voice a squeaky falsetto, she said, "Let me out! Let me out! That's what he's saying."

"What he's saying is—let me alone."

Then she put her hand down to touch his head. "It feels like rubber," she said, laughing. "Come here and touch him."

Unable to shake off the memory of the dying humpback and blood in the water, seeing those terrible teeth close up, I said, "Go right ahead, Angie. He can take your feet off in one bite."

"Sure he can," she said, "but he isn't going to do it, are you, pretty boy?"

Then the blackfish withdrew from the rock and swam away, edging along the nets again.

I sat down. "Angie, I swear you are insane." I couldn't imagine anyone doing what she'd just done. It was as bad as walking that building ledge naked.

She dropped down beside me again and laughed, as much to herself as to me. "You know, I didn't have any idea he'd come to me. I just yelled at him for the heck of it. But these things must have some brain-power. Something that big having a thinking brain! You know, I bet I could even train it."

Maybe. But I said, "Don't do it here. All we want is to collect the money."

Angie said, "You know, the psychic part of my D.B. tells me that these blackfish are from Admiralty Inlet."

I said, "They could be from Queen Charlotte Strait, they could be from Johnstone Strait, they could be from the Strait of Georgia. Angie, you don't know where they come from."

She put her hand to her forehead and closed her eyes, like mind readers do. "I see them now. They came through the Strait of Juan de Fuca, between Cape Flattery and Vancouver Island twelve days ago, threading the ship traffic. In the gloom behind them were the skyscrapers of Seattle and ahead were grim, gray North Pacific skies. They swam westward, then turned north past Swiftsure Bank Lightship—"

I interrupted, "Angie, you're full of B.S. as well as D.B."

She pealed off laughter, then began staring at the blackfish again, which was now swimming back toward the middle of the cove. She said, "Okay, tell me what's going to happen."

I told her what I knew about the ex-movie star and Ocean Arena. "He'll buy it if it's as big as we say, and healthy."

"For a hundred thousand dollars?"

"Yep."

"Jamie, I'm ashamed of you," she said.

I was open-mouthed. I didn't even ask her why she was ashamed of me.

"You saw that thing on TV about ocean parks?"

I had. "Yeah."

"So they'll make this beautiful animal squirt water on people. They'll make him jump up in the air. They'll put a bridle on him so someone can ride him. And the worst thing of all, they'll probably make him open his mouth so a chimpanzee dressed up like a dentist can brush his teeth."

"What's wrong with all that?"

"It's an insult, that's what!" She nodded over toward the blackfish. "Anything that big and beautiful shouldn't have to be a clown."

I gave up. Next she'd say to stop circuses. They had performing animals. Next she'd say to stop horse races. I said, quietly and calmly, "All we want to do is sell him."

"And what will you do with all that money?"

I told her that part. Maui. Dirt bike. New boat. Move to Prince Rupert.

"You've got it all planned?"

"More or less."

Angie yawned. "I have to think about this."

"About what?"

"About whether you should take the hundred thousand or turn him loose."

It was none of her business! I said, "Angie, that's not for you to decide. It's up to us."

Ignoring that advice, she said, "I'm sleepy. See you later." She got up, then jumped down off the rock and plodded back through the woods toward Lumber Landing.

I watched her disappear into the narrow darkness of the trail, swallowed up by the tall trees. She should have been happy that we were going to change our lives.

I sat awhile longer, thinking of what Angie had said, then got up and went over near the edge of the rock to wait for the blackfish to surface again. When the big snout broke water I yelled, "Hey, clown, come over here!" But the only response was a wet whoosh from the blowhole, then he slid back under the water to keep up his lazy patrol of Wilwilli Cove.

Maybe Angie had a magic touch with animals. She seemed to have it with people. But her being psychic was nonsense.

About fifteen minutes later the *Dawn Girl* chugged up, and the first thing I said to Papa was, "Angie thinks we ought to turn him loose." It was the wrong thing to say.

Papa was outraged. "That Portogee girl is out of her mind, an' it's none of her business what we do with this blackfish." It was not the first time he'd made judgment on Angie. He fumed. "Turn him loose?" I didn't mention Anette Debar.

Then I said, "You know what she did? She called him right up to the rock and patted him on the head."

"I don't believe that!"

"She did it."

Papa shook his head in amazement. "It's a wonder she didn't lose her arm."

"That's what I told her."

Papa said angrily, "Well, if she comes back an' I'm not here, you tell her to stay the hell away from Wilwilli an' this blackfish. I'll tell Cristo the same thing as soon as I see him."

With Angie Pinheiro, that wouldn't do any good at all.

It took us almost two hours to unload the boat, set up camp, and rig three portable lights that would operate off the ginny during the short, late June period of darkness. Two were aimed along the netting, along the line between South Rock and the one to the north. The other would flood the cove. They were most often used at the Landing when someone had to work on an engine at night.

About two-thirty in the afternoon the CB carried Mama's voice on the receiver. "Per, a helicopter from Port Hardy just landed here. What about that? Like to blew all the shingles off the houses. That Mr. Cooke, a Mr. Tebbetts, and a Dr. Greenlee are here in the kitchen having coffee. They want to see the blackfish. I'll tell you that helicopter woke the woods up. The dogs are still barking."

"Be right there," said Papa.

In a moment he'd untied the boat and headed back for the Landing, leaving me to watch the whale, a task I was beginning to enjoy less and less. In these times, alone with that big fish, I tried to make myself think of the beach at Maui, the dirt bike, and school this fall in Rupert. Out of prison!

14

*N*ever had I seen a real movie star five feet away, even an old one who appears only on the late-lates, and I must say that tall, tanned Zachary Cooke was not dressed the way we do it in B.C. He was wearing white jeans and a gold chain was around his neck. A red shirt was beneath a white nylon golf jacket, and I also noticed white moccasins with little gold tassels on his feet. No socks. So Hollywood had come to Wilwilli Cove, which was not even on B.C. maps.

Along with him was a short, stocky blond man named Georgie Tebbetts and a bespectacled white-haired man, milk-white beard to match, named Doc Greenlee. Papa introduced me to them, saying that I'd helped catch the blackfish.

We were all standing on South Rock, watching our whale swim lazily around, paying no attention to us. Had he known what the plans were he might have been swimming a little faster and thinking about plowing through the nets.

Cooke wanted to know about the size. "Anyone ever seen a bigger one, anywhere?"

Doc Greenlee was a veterinarian, an international expert on the care of killer whales. He answered, "May be bigger ones around but I doubt it. He's probably seven, eight tons. My guess is that he's around twenty-five years old." Doc Greenlee himself was seventy-two, beginning to shrivel, but spry enough.

Georgie Tebbetts turned out to be the chief trainer for Ocean Arena. With short cropped hair, he looked like a professional swimmer, and that's what he was, an ex-Navy UDT man. A huge Toshiba waterproof watch, with all kinds of gadgets on it, was on his left wrist. An old-fashioned hearing-aid button was in his left ear, hooked to a receiver in his shirt pocket. Georgie Tebbetts looked to be the same age as Papa, but he was a small man instead of a fullback.

"Okay, how long is it?" Cooke asked, probably thinking about how the blackfish would look when performing in the biggest killer-whale tank in the world.

"Well, he's over twenty-five feet is my guess," said Doc Greenlee.

Papa caught my eye and nodded, grinning. We'd certainly qualified on that condition.

"How much over twenty-five feet?" asked Cooke, sounding a little annoyed.

I was beginning to dislike him.

Georgie Tebbetts answered, "Only way to really know is to put a tape measure on him, and I'm not ready for that at present."

Cooke threw up his hands in exasperation. "All right, can you great experts tell me what kind of shape he's in? We're looking at a major investment for the studio."

Doc Greenlee squinted at Cooke from under the

brim of his orange porkpie hat, his curly white hair sticking out like a halo around the orange. "I've been here only five minutes and I can't tell you what kind of shape he's in aside from the fact that he's alive and looks fine. We'll watch him for a day or two and then I'll give you my best estimate. I can give you blood-test results after we get to California. If you want me to do an electrocardiogram on him, that may take a month or never. It'll depend on how well Georgie gets along with him. I wouldn't ask anybody to put a sensor on any animal this size without getting to know him."

I thought about telling them what Angie had done, then thought better of it. Later, maybe.

Tebbetts, intently watching the slow movement of the giant dorsal fin, said to Cooke, "I just know we'd be better off with a younger, smaller animal. This one is going to be very rough to train—maybe impossible."

My heart sank and Papa frowned.

Before I could say what Angie had done, Cooke turned swiftly on Tebbetts. "Look, Georgie, for the tenth time, we need the biggest one in the world! That's why we're here. The only reason."

That promptly ended that discussion.

Just then Desdemona and Persephone broke surface and whistled a few times.

Papa said, "Those are the other two I was talking about. They been pestering us along the nets ever since we caught the big one."

Georgie said, "They sound a little agitated."

Doc Greenlee studied them a moment and then said, "Those two are females."

So Angie had guessed right. She didn't know anything more about blackfish than I did and this was another example of her extraordinary luck.

Doc Greenlee laughed softly. "He's got a pair of lovers. He likes to have that glossy back rubbed, and I guarantee those two ladies know how to do it."

Right down Angie's alley.

We all kept watching the females for a minute or so, then turned back to the killer in the cove.

Worried about feeding it, also missing the entire sockeye opening, which we could not afford to do, Papa said, "Things bein' equal, gentlemen, how long do you think it'll be before you know you want to buy this fish?"

Doc Greenlee took his time in answering. "Oh, forty-eight hours, I'd say. Day after tomorrow. We want to see if he has any wounds or infections. Georgie'll get in the water with him tomorrow to see how he acts. Never can tell. He may be a wild horse."

Again I fought back the temptation to tell them about Angie. Papa had no such reservations. He said, "A girl coaxed him up to the rock earlier today and patted him on the head."

Doc Greenlee went "Hmm."

Tebbetts said, "Well, that sounds promising. She had a lot of guts."

I said, "She does that."

Papa said, "You know, Mr. Cooke, it's gonna be getting expensive to feed him. He'll do two hundred pounds a day, an' I can't get it cheaper than a dime over wholesale."

"Don't worry about it. Just buy what you need and AFE will take care of it."

Papa was relieved, I could tell. AFE was American Film Enterprises, we learned.

Then Cooke added, dramatically, "And from now on all of us will refer to this bizarre creature of the deep as Tyrannus. T-y-r-a-n-n-u-s."

What's a tyrannus? I thought.

Tebbetts said that name sounded like a dinosaur.

Cooke smiled, pleased with himself, replying, "A name I just made up. Fits, doesn't it?"

Doc Greenlee cleared his throat. "You've done some homework, Zachary. That name goes back to the Romans. *Tyrannus balaearum* or *formidabilissimus balaearum hostis*. Scientists nowadays call it simply *Orcinus orca.*"

Cooke waved all that away, saying, "It fits, doesn't it? Biggest killer whale in the world for the biggest oceanarium tank in the world. Great for publicity. Great for TV clips. Billboards. Come to Ocean Arena and see Mighty Tyrannus."

Doc Greenlee shrugged.

Papa laughed awkwardly, looking over at me. "All right with us whatever you call him. Isn't that right, Jamie?"

As long as they bought the whale, they could call him Mount McKinley. "Sure," I said.

So now we had Tyrannus, Persephone, and Desdemona at Wilwilli. I could just hear the other skippers at the Landing laughing. "Ty-who?" They always called a herring a herring, a blackfish a blackfish. Fishermen would be laughing for miles around. But they wouldn't laugh so much after we cashed the check.

Cooke looked at Tyrannus once more, saying, "I'm really not of any use here while you people make up your minds." He then scanned the makeshift camp we'd set up about fifty feet away from the rock. He wasn't the camping-out type. "Why don't I go back to Port Hardy and stay there until you call me? I need to keep in touch with the studio, anyway."

"That's a very good idea, Zachary," Doc Greenlee said.

"All right with you, Georgie?"

Tebbetts said, "Fine with me, Zach."

Cooke then asked Papa, "Can you get me back to that chopper?"

"Easy."

Cooke broke into a big grin, happy that he could eat in a restaurant that night, sleep on a good mattress. "Anything you men need from civilization?"

Tebbetts shook his head. "If Mr. Tidd can get us two sleeping bags, we'll be fine."

"Sensational," said Cooke. "Just take good care of Tyrannus for me."

A moment later the *Dawn Girl* headed back for the Landing. About a half hour later, in the quietness, we heard the chopper engine start and then finally saw it lift off over the trees, heading southwest.

The blackfish had begun to talk again. "You understand any of that?" I asked Doc Greenlee.

"All I know is that they've got at least ten different sounds. I can tell an up-scream from a down-scream, a click burst from a whine, chatter from buzzes."

"Does anybody understand them?"

" 'Anybody' meaning humans? Not yet. Someday we will. Quite a few scientists are trying hard, learning the frequencies and modulations. Sooner or later we'll communicate with them in their language."

"Talk back and forth?"

"I think so. Computers will sort out the patterns, then we'll start to understand some things."

"You think they're almost human?"

"I wouldn't go as far as 'almost,' but all mammals are partially human. His blood is very much like yours. From a medical standpoint, he has most of the same aches and pains you do. He can have stomach ulcers, anemia, pneumonia, cancer, kidney failure, flu . . ."

Turning to look at Tyrannus, I wondered just how human he really was.

I guess Angie couldn't contain her curiosity about the visitors. She came up the wood's path to Wilwilli and I introduced her, saying she was the girl who had touched the blackfish. I explained who they were.

Tebbetts said, admiringly, "Maybe you ought to stay up here and help me."

Angie replied, flatly, "I want nothing to do with this."

"C'mon, Angie," I said. She sounded downright hostile.

Doc Greenlee laughed. "Stick around, you might learn something about this big fellow."

Angie looked at the old man in the porkpie hat, snapping, "I hope I'll learn you've turned him loose."

I said to them, "She's just upset."

Angie swung her head toward me. "That, I am."

Doc Greenlee nodded. "I understand."

Tebbetts said, "So do I."

"Then why are you here?" Angie asked, still hostile.

Tebbetts answered, quietly, "It's the way I make my living."

Doc Greenlee said it was the same for him.

Angie took another look at the blackfish, shook her head in disgust, and went back into the woods.

I apologized for her but the experts said that wasn't necessary. They'd run into people like Angie before.

15

In late afternoon, standing outside the tent, Tebbetts was readying to put on his work outfit. On his thighs were red and blue tattoos from Navy days. One said "UDT 2" and the matching tattoo said "UDT 5," underwater demolition teams in which he'd served. After an explosion at eighteen fathoms off Cuba, Georgie had retired from the Navy with a hearing disability at the age of thirty. He was now seven years beyond that.

"I've spent as much time in the water as out of it," he said, tugging on a "leakproof" dry suit, the kind often used in northern waters. But they always leaked a little. After Tebbetts left the Navy he went to work for Sea World, down in San Diego, learning how to train blackfish.

"Zach Cooke offered me a job as chief trainer at this new one and I took it. More money."

There wasn't much skin diving up this way compared with California. Even in midsummer the water was cold enough to make goose bumps into mountains.

I kept on watching him. "You going in the water now?"

"Nope. Just want him to see me in this suit so when I do go in tomorrow he'll know it's me." He added, with a slight smile, "I hope he knows it's me."

His duffel bag contained more diving gear than street clothes. Flippers, hood, face mask, gloves and bootees so his hands and feet wouldn't go numb right away.

"Training blackfish more dangerous than being in the UDTs?"

"I should say not, as long as that thing"—he pointed at Tyrannus—"doesn't declare war on you."

I asked how long it took to train one.

"Depends strictly on the animal. They may start responding in a week, but to do all the tricks takes months."

"You ever stick your head in their mouths?" I'd seen trainers do that on TV.

"Sure. But you better know your whale and he better know you. And it's not my favorite way to spend ten seconds. They tend to have bad breath."

"You're never scared?"

Glancing up at me, and then over at Tyrannus, he said, "Have been. They get moody and grumpy. Have tantrums. An animal that big in a nasty mood is something you stay away from."

"One ever attacked you?"

"Once. I went into the tank without a wet suit and Lummie took me to the bottom. He was playing, but he still took me down there and pinned me."

"For how long?"

"Twenty, thirty seconds. Then he let go. I never went in again without a wet suit."

I had a quick mental picture of Georgie down on the bottom, held by the blackfish.

"They ever attack anyone out here?" I asked.

"You mean in the ocean?"

I nodded.

"Only time I know about was off Point Sur, down in California. One got a surfer and it cost him ninety stitches. I'd say if they come around, get up on the beach for safety's sake."

There wasn't any surfing up our way and no one from the Landing got into the water on purpose. Some lunatics up around Prince Rupert did scuba diving and they deserved to be bitten by blackfish.

"You married?"

"Yep. Have a boy about your age, in fact."

"What does he think about you training killer whales?"

Tebbetts grinned. "He thinks I'm a little weird."

Soon, Tebbetts was sitting on the edge of the rock, where he could easily be seen by Tyrannus, a dozen or more fat salmon beside him. The way to friendship is through the belly.

I flopped down beside Doc Greenlee. "You been with Mr. Cooke a long time?"

"Six-thirty this morning," he said. "Never knew he existed until the day before yesterday."

"You treat other animals? Dogs, cats, horses?"

He shook his head. "Just sea mammals. Mostly for aquariums or these entertainment places like Cooke is opening."

"I never knew there were people to doctor black-fish."

"Not many of us," Doc Greenlee said. "One morning about twenty-five years ago I got a call from a zoo asking if I'd look at a sick elephant seal. I'd never even seen one close up. But you get into all kinds of things by accident."

I was starting to ask if he had to get down into the water to treat a blackfish but he held up a hand and said, "Ss-ssh."

The blunt head surfaced near South Rock and Tebbetts began whistling and buzzing, imitating killer-whale talk. He tossed a salmon toward Tyrannus and it went down in a single gulp. Then the big head slid under again, one eye zeroed on Tebbetts.

Doc Greenlee was from Tacoma, Washington, near Seattle. And, yes, even old as he was, he did go into the water to treat his patients. But he used a bow and arrow and darts for routine injections. Vitamins and such.

What had been puzzling me since Tuesday was why that blackfish didn't go through our nets like a freight train.

Plain, ordinary sonar was Doc's answer, just like Papa was told, the same thing the Navy used to track subs. "He clicks in a series of nasal sacs located in his head and these sacs run right into his forehead, which we call the 'melon.' Then the clicks bounce off whatever obstruction is ahead. Just ordinary echolocation. He's got a built-in computer that tells him the direction and distance, but the thing the computer doesn't tell him is what the substance is."

"The nets?"

"Could be concrete too. For reasons none of us know, nets really confuse them. Not being solid, they give off confusing signals and the animals surrender. They don't even try to jump up or ram the nets."

"I'd always thought they were so smart."

"They are. The Navy has sent 'em down a thousand feet to recover objects off the bottom, but they still can't tell the difference between concrete and nets."

Tyrannus surfaced again, to be greeted by more chatter from Tebbetts, who this time held the sockeye by its tail, inviting the whale to come over and take it. There was a swish and Georgie released the sockeye. It disappeared within a split second down that crocodile opening. There was a clack as the jaws closed.

Meanwhile, Doc Greenlee had been watching the females and said to Tebbetts, "Make you a bet those two are in the family way and he's the papa."

"No bets," said the UDT man.

Babies! I wish he hadn't told me that. "What makes you think they're pregnant?"

"My eyes. Cows, horses, people, killer whales all get fat around the gut."

"How do you know they're his?"

"Well, I don't see any other bulls out there. Do you?"

Thinking again of what the killer did to the humpty, I said, "In here, he seems so gentle."

Doc Greenlee replied, "Well, I'll tell you the most quoted description of him—'He's got the appetite of a hog, the cruelty of a wolf, the courage of a bulldog, and the most terrible jaws afloat!' Cut those nets, let him loose, and he's a Tyrannus all right, a breathtaking killer."

Doc Greenlee added, "But I've also seen an orca lick Georgie's cheek with that long tongue. Right, Georgie?"

The trainer looked back at us briefly. "I won't let all of them do that, and any time one gives me a whistle that sounds like a cross between a rusty hinge and a mockingbird, I get out. Fast!"

"That means he's ready to attack?"

"People come away from my shows saying how sweet and gentle they are, but I don't get into a tank with one unless I have a backup with an oxygen tank. If one takes me down, I want someone there to stick a tube into my mouth until I can reason with that animal."

"Can you do that? Reason with them?"

Doc Greenlee said, "Listen, their brains are *physically* as well developed as yours. There's an indication of memory. He can think, to an extent."

In a few minutes Doc Greenlee began using a stopwatch to check the whale's breathing intervals and Tebbetts kept talking to him in buzzes and whistles while feeding him the sockeye meat.

Papa soon brought the *Dawn Girl* back with borrowed sleeping bags and hot food for the evening meal. Papa said that, while he was at the Landing, Cooke unclasped a gold money clip and gave him five one-hundred-dollar bills to buy food for Tyrannus. Until that evening my father had never held five hundred-dollar bills in his hands. He said he felt a thrill just holding them.

Then Papa had asked Cooke for a favor. Have that roll of film with the leaping blackfish on it developed in Port Hardy.

I went home an hour later to spend the night in my own bed. Papa had given up the tent to the visitors and was going to sleep on the *Dawn Girl* in that single bunk. No thanks.

On the way to my house I stopped by Angie's to tell

her she was right about Desdemona and Persephone. A dumb thing to do.

I refused to go inside and stood out on the porch.

Old Cristo was still up. I could hear him in there, talking in Portuguese to Mrs. Pinheiro. As far as I was concerned, he could go jump into Wilwilli Cove and let Tyrannus gnaw on him. On the other hand, Old Cristo might be inedible, like trash fish.

Angie had on a woolen nightgown and big fluffy pink slippers. Her long hair had been divided into two big braids. I'd never seen her this way. She wasn't so glamorous.

"So they're pregnant. Now you've got to turn that whale loose. I'll help you and your papa will never know."

I looked around, blowing out a chill breath. "I wish I hadn't come here."

"I would have found out sooner or later."

"How?"

"By looking at their bellies! Go over and look at Anette Debar."

I said, "Stop talking about letting that blackfish loose. You know what he means to us. Our whole lives will change."

Angie said, "So will his. How'd you like to be locked up the rest of your life?" She paused. "You already told me. Napoleon!"

"Angie, there are zoos all over the world that have animals in them for people to enjoy. What should we do, close all the zoos? And circuses and racetracks? Padlock Sea World?"

"Maybe," she said, nodding. "Wait a minute. Maybe that's a good idea, Jamie. Close all the zoos. Let all the animals loose. Absolutely."

"What about that blackfish in Sealand? He's cooped up. Turn him loose?"

"Yep."

"You do have a diseased brain," I said.

She grinned back. "I'm happy with it."

"By the way," I said, "the big one has a name now. Tyrannus."

"That's a good name for a Japanese monster movie. Why not call him Wilwilli? Or just Willi?"

"It's a show-business name. That's what he's going to be in. Show business. A star."

"Yeah," Angie said, with distaste. "Yeah, I saw that dyed-hair ham actor when the chopper came in here this afternoon. His nose went into a sniff when he smelled the cannery stink. You ever see any of his movies? They're awful."

"He's a producer now," I said, trying to defend him.

"He's a horse's banana," Angie said.

I said, "You're just mad about everything."

She answered, "Yeah! We're going out in the morning, but I'll talk to you day after tomorrow."

"About what?"

"About Tyrannus, of course."

"No thanks."

She went back inside and I went on home.

I finally had to put myself to sleep thinking about all the money that was just around the corner. In the next room Mama was doing the same.

Next morning, at breakfast, she said, "I had trouble sleeping, Jamie. You know, I haven't worn a bathing suit since we lived in Vancouver. That man at the motel down the block used to let us swim in his heated pool. Remember?"

I remembered. "You'll look fine."

She poured herself another cup of coffee. "I'm so skinny I'll never look fine. Pipe legs."

"Better than being fat, isn't it?"

"I don't know."

"I like you like you are," I said.

"See how white I am." She lifted the sleeve of her sweatshirt. "I walk out on that beach and I'll look like a defeathered pigeon."

She was always so self-conscious.

"People aren't going to be watching you."

"I hope not," she said, sighing.

"Do you think all the zoos should be closed? That's what I was thinking about last night."

"What?" She frowned, giving me a puzzled look. "Close all the zoos? That would be terrible. People learn about animals in zoos. How else would you enjoy monkeys or polar bears?"

I nodded. "But how do you think *they* feel? Being in captivity?"

"There's no way to ask them, but I think they like it. Long as they get plenty of food and good shelter—" She stopped abruptly, struck by a thought. Or maybe it was a guess. "Is this another Angie Pinheiro debate?"

"Kind of."

Mama laughed softly. She liked Angie, as did most everyone in Lumber Landing, but Angie could get people, including Mama, stirred up pretty quickly. "What was it last summer?"

"Indian fishing rights." She'd written to a half dozen newspapers saying Indians should have special and unlimited salmon rights. The letter sounded as if it had been written by a boat captain. She signed it

"A. Pinheiro." The Native Brotherhood were overjoyed.

"I thought Cristo blew her into the water on that one. I know he was wild," said Mama.

"She doesn't stay down long."

Mama stared at me a moment. "What she's really after is our whale, isn't she?"

I nodded.

"Is she serious?"

"I think so."

"Well, tell her to steer clear. That's a message from me, over and above what your father told Cristo. And in case she doesn't know it, I've heard that dolphins like contact with humans and that killer whale is dolphin family."

"You think they like captivity?"

"That's what I heard. I've also seen it, Jamie. They have fun doing those tricks down at Sea World. I saw that with my own eyes. Doing high jumps and riding people around on their backs. It seemed to me they enjoyed the applause."

I left it at that. But I wondered how anyone would know that dolphins would rather be in tanks than out at sea.

Mama leaned forward in her chair and stared at me a moment, lowering her voice. "Jamie, this may be our only chance to get your papa off the sea, off boats."

I frowned back at her. He'd already told me what kind of boat he planned to buy—a Bristol Bay, with Teleflex steering, Seascan radar, and a Gemtronics sounder. I said, "He's planning on buying a new boat."

"I'm going to work on him, Jamie. I want you both

off the sea. I don't want to be a widow again. January almost killed me with fright. If I lost you . . ."

"But fishing is all Papa knows how to do."

"That's all he thinks he knows how to do. He's a good mechanic. He can take some of that money and open a garage. Maybe open a seafood market? Maybe open an auto parts store?"

Oh, my. I hadn't known what she was plotting all along, thinking far beyond Maui.

"Help me, Jamie. You don't want to fish the rest of your life, do you?"

I had to be truthful. "No."

"Well . . ."

"But he really loves it out there, Mama. We've talked about it."

"He just thinks he loves it. He's never tried anything else."

That was also true. He'd grown up fishing with Grandpa Tidd. But it was hard for me to picture him behind a counter, selling auto parts. He'd close the door and lock it on the opening day of sockeye fishing.

"Help me, will you?"

I nodded, feeling uncomfortable about it, and said I had to get back to the cove.

As I was going out the door Mama called out, "Jamie, we *need* that money. We *need* it."

I looked back and nodded again. We *did* need the money, all right. For a lot of things beyond Maui.

16

Greenlee mused, "One thing is sure. He doesn't know fear, doesn't know what it is. A tiger or a lion knows fear. This animal doesn't. Now, I'm sure he knows we humans are different. Knows we aren't fish or animals. But knowing that we *are* different, he doesn't know that we are also deadly. He doesn't know that we're his only true enemy."

Tebbetts was already dressed in his dry suit. Today he was wearing longies underneath it. He finished up by putting on the bootees before pulling custom fins over his feet. It was about ten in the morning and partially sunny.

I asked what he'd do when he got into the water.

"Get acquainted, I hope. I've done this in tanks a number of times, met a whale for the first time, but never in the animal's own territory. There may be a difference, but I hope he'll remember me from yesterday." About thirty sockeye had been laid out on the rock under wet burlap.

I looked over at Tyrannus. Fifty or so feet from the nets, he was moving slowly by them toward the north end of the cove. He hadn't grown any during the

night, but suddenly he seemed to be the size of a box-
car.

Doc Greenlee was carefully watching the blackfish
too. "Georgie, if you think he's nervous, come back
out in a hurry. There's no rush to this."

Papa, who'd gone to the buy barge at Kwiklit for
more of the deluxe diet, wouldn't have agreed about
there being no rush. There was a great big hurry as
far as he was concerned. Getting that check was all he
was thinking about.

Fixing the turtleneck collar of his suit, Tebbetts
said, almost to himself, "I don't know how he'll re-
act."

Doc Greenlee said, "Just take it real slow and easy,
Georgie. He may never have seen a human swimmer."

There was no backup man with an oxygen tank
standing by. Tebbetts was on his own.

Doc Greenlee said, "You know better than me,
Georgie, but if he starts along the net toward those
females, I'd stay away from him. He may think you've
got some sweetheart ideas. Try to stay close here, let
him come to you."

"I intend to do just that," said Tebbetts, looking
bleakly at the vet.

After wetting and tugging on his flippers, he spit
into the face mask and rubbed it to keep it from fog-
ging, then backed off South Rock, splashing into the
water on his shoulders, turning quickly to keep one
hand firmly onshore.

Doc Greenlee said softly, "Stay by me in case we
have to jerk him out."

I nodded.

Almost in a whisper, Doc Greenlee said, "This animal can see a hundred feet, laterally, just beneath the surface, where the light penetrates. If he lifts his head above the surface, he has a cat's day vision. Only the bat has better hearing."

Tyrannus not only heard the splash but, using that hundred-foot vision underwater skidded immediately across the cove and came up beside Georgie, whooshing.

Slowly treading in the water, clinging with one hand to the rock, Tebbetts whistled a few times.

You can hold your breath with your mouth open, and I think I did that morning. Even the ravens stopped cawing.

We could see only the back of Tebbetts's neoprene-hooded head, a black dome. He was facing into the cove, left hand on the rock, right one slightly extended, as if he was saying hello to the whale. With that eight-ton body only three feet away, Georgie Tebbetts looked like he was a tiny waterbug.

I was still holding my breath. What we might be seeing in a few seconds was the eating of a live human being. Two or three bites at most.

One big orca eye seemed to be studying the waterbug making these clicks and whistles. Also visible were most of the forty-odd interlocking teeth. Mouth about one third open, the conical chewing machines appeared to be sharp and in fine shape. His tongue lay like a slab of underdone turkey meat, pinkish on the top and sides, level with his bottom row of teeth.

We heard Tebbetts saying to Tyrannus, in human language, "How you doin', old boy?" The words seemed to be forced out, through his teeth. He said later that he'd wet his dry suit when Tyrannus's right eye came within six inches of his face. Then he clicked some more in whale language.

Doc Greenlee whispered, "Don't move! Don't distract him."

I made myself into a statue.

Then Tebbetts said, still facing the blunt head, "Doc, go very slowly, but get me a big sockeye and put it into my right hand."

Doc said quietly, "You sure he won't take your whole arm?"

Tebbetts answered, as if someone were standing on his chest, "I'm not sure of anything. I'm about to drown in my own sweat."

Doc Greenlee made a gradual move across the rock with a big sockeye, placing the tail in Georgie's hand, and no sooner did Doc draw back than there was a flash of black and white. The great jaws opened and the salmon was gone, leaving Tebbetts with his right hand poised in the air, as if trying to catch a taxi.

Tebbetts said, "God Almighty, why did I ever get into this business?"

The whale circled away from the black waterbug up against the rock.

"Let's do it again, Doc," Tebbetts said. "The one thing I don't want is for this fellow to be hungry."

Over the next hour, while we watched, Tebbetts stayed in the water, feeding the blackfish a salmon now and then, talking to him, sometimes in English, sometimes in killer-whale language. He was touching the eight tons now and then.

Doc whispered, "He hears as well underwater as he does above."

I said, "What could the whale hear down there?"

"Are you kidding? That's about the noisiest place on

earth. Sound travels four times faster in water than it does in air. You wouldn't believe the noise at the three-fathom curve. Other whales clicking. Fish and shrimp jabbering. Small rocks chipping up against each other. Moans and howls and shrieks down there. Ship and boat propellers. Oil pumps thudding away. A lot of stuff that floats is always tinkling and bumping around. There's constant bedlam and babble down there."

Tebbetts broke in, "Jamie, go over to the tent and look in my duffel bag. There's a long-handled scrub brush. Bring it here."

I found the brush and placed it in Tebbetts's hand.

"Watch now," said Doc Greenlee.

The whale had seemed much less anxious to eat when Georgie had given him the last sockeye, and when he stayed in position for a moment, Tebbetts kicked off from the rock and went alongside the black and white body, dwarfed by it, and then reached out with the brush.

Doc Greenlee explained quietly, "They love it. It's like scratching a flea-bitten dog's belly."

Sure enough, Tyrannus shivered with delight, exactly the way a dog does, as the stiff brush caressed his back.

Doc Greenlee murmured, "That's just about all the brownie points Georgie needs."

Slowly treading water, his right hip up against the side of the whale, Tebbetts said, "I think we're going to be friends."

Doc Greenlee said, "I haven't seen any wounds on him."

Scrubbing away, Tebbetts said, "Not a one."

"That mean he's okay?" I asked.

"Means just what we just said."

Tebbetts soon came out of the water to rest and sat down on South Rock for a conference with Doc Greenlee. Pulling off his hood and face mask, leaving red marks on his forehead and cheeks, he said, "I think he may be trainable. He's really too old to start playing a lot of games, but then again he might enjoy them. The more I'm around these creatures, the less I really know about them."

"Amen to that," said Doc Greenlee.

Tebbetts closed his eyes, water puddling all around his body as the underwater suit dripped. He'd been through an ordeal. He just sat there, eyes closed, breathing deeply.

Aside from the whoosh of the whale, the bird noises, it got very quiet in the cove.

Doc Greenlee shook his head a little, watching Tyrannus swim. Finally he said, a faraway, absent look in his eyes, "They're so very, very old, Jamie. Even before the Stone Age."

I didn't respond.

Tebbetts lowered his back to the rock, saying nothing, just resting. He put his left wrist over his eyes.

I said to Doc Greenlee, "Why do you think they know we're different?"

"You just saw it. He didn't make a meal out of Georgie. He permitted Georgie to enter his world."

Eyes still closed, Tebbetts spoke up. "I think they really want to establish a relationship with us. We offer them a chance to use those brains Doc was talking about."

I don't know why I shivered when Tebbetts said that—us offering them a chance to use their brains. I did, and remember it to this day. "You said we were their only enemy."

"We are," said Doc Greenlee.

Then I asked him what he thought about closing all the zoos down.

He laughed. "I've thought about that very thing. It would be fine if we could get all the people into the cages. As long as the people are out, the animals are worse off than in the zoos."

Tebbetts joined the laughter and then stood up, slipping back into the water a moment later.

"You serious?"

"Well, no," said Doc Greenlee. "I really don't want to put people in cages—not all of them. But year before last in Africa some poachers were using a leftover Vietnam gunship to get elephant tusks. Be nice to have those kinds in cages."

"*A*fter you do all this, what's next?"

"Not much up here," said Doc Greenlee. "When we get him back to California, if we get him there, I'll do blood tests, electrocardiogram, oxygen analysis, and other things. All we want to do now is make sure he's reasonably healthy and not too skittish. These people are investing more than a quarter million in this animal. That's why they hired me to say yes or no."

If they were going to pay us a hundred thousand, where did the other money come in? "Why so much?"

"We'll have to build a floating pen for him, tow him to Vancouver, put him down in a sheepskin hammock, keep his skin wet all the way, lift him up into a jet, hook him to a respirator, and *pray*. Orcas are voluntary breathers, not involuntary like us. They aren't as tough as they look."

"Any doubt you'll get him to California?"

Doc Greenlee lifted his snowy brows. "You take a whale from the sea and he's scared to death. That's why I said no to a helicopter lift from here to Vancouver, even if it could be arranged. He could go into psychogenic shock."

"What's that?"

"Mental shock. You have to give him better treatment than any human you're flying."

Tebbetts was still in the water with Tyrannus when the *Dawn Girl* returned with more sockeyes. Papa had stopped at the Landing to pick up my mother.

She said, "I don't believe my eyes," when she saw Tebbetts swimming around in Wilwilli Cove with the whale.

I said, "He's been doing that all morning."

Papa said, "I'd jus' as soon jump in with a great white shark."

Doc Greenlee said, "Oh, no, you wouldn't!"

Everybody was in an up mood.

Tebbetts, treading water again, hooked his arm on the dorsal fin as the whale came by and was towed forty or fifty feet. Tebbetts let go and came up spurting water, laughing. He shouted, "Mr. Tidd, he's fooled me. I think you got yourself a good animal here."

Papa grinned. "I sure hope so." Each day that he hadn't fished had brought more concern. We were losing several thousand a day by not drifting our nets. If Tyrannus wasn't bought, disaster.

Doc Greenlee said, "Okay, I'll put you out of your misery. Get me through to Zachary Cooke."

Papa's grin widened. "Will I ever?"

In a moment he was calling the Bella Bella marine operator on the single side-band and asking for Port Hardy Inn. When he was patched into that place on Granville Street he turned the mike over to Doc Greenlee.

Zachary Cooke's voice came in.

Doc Greenlee said, "I've got some good news. This

whale seems to be very healthy—no hundred percent guarantee—but we think he's healthy. Also, Georgie has changed his mind. He's big and he's old, but he's trainable, Georgie thinks."

Papa's whole face was a gigantic grin, stretching back to his ears. Mama was nodding, tears welling in her eyes. No more Januaries. Me? No more Lumber Landing! No more waiting for a bear to eat me. No more correspondence courses. I could hardly contain a yell that Zachary Cooke would have heard in Port Hardy without the help of the radio.

Cooke asked, "What do we do now?"

Doc Greenlee answered, "Come and get us. Georgie and I talked about it last night. We'll get the sea pen built in Port Hardy, tow it back here, and then get this animal to Vancouver. Charter us an Air Canada freighter to Los Angeles, and we're in business."

"Great," said Cooke. "I told that chopper pilot I'd probably need him tomorrow. I'll see if I can't get him over here this afternoon. I found a couple of good places to eat. We'll celebrate tonight."

"Nothing wrong with the way we've been eating," said Doc Greenlee, to make Mama feel good about the last two days.

Then the director of Ocean Arena said, "Put Perry Tidd on."

Papa took the mike.

"Perry, I got those pictures developed yesterday. They're sensational, and I want to buy them."

Surprised that any picture he shot could be sensational, Papa said, "You don't need to buy them. Just get another set made for me. I'll pay for 'em."

"You don't understand," said the movie producer. "These pictures'll knock your head off. There's one here with that killer fifteen feet in the air, coming down on that other big whale. I want the exclusive rights to all of them. I'll give you five hundred."

Papa laughed feebly. Riches were beginning to rain down on him. "Five hundred for some pitchers I shot, I don't believe it."

"Wait'll you see 'em."

Papa kept laughing and shaking his head. "All right then, I'll take your money, Mr. Cooke. I'd like a set for myself."

"Five sets, Perry. Ten sets!"

Papa signed off, saying, "Lace, what in the world is happenin' to us? It's like that blackfish is turnin' everythin' to gold."

I'd never seen his sea-whipped face so lit up. He'd worked so hard all his life.

Mama came over to him and put her arms around him, saying, "Per, we deserve it. We do deserve it. We do." They kissed. I almost got teary-eyed.

Then she hugged me, grinning widely. "Our luck has changed, Jamie. Isn't that wonderful?"

Yes, it was. Not the least of it was that she'd never have to put those long legs into short-shorts again. And maybe Papa would leave the sea.

Yet, somewhere in the back of my head was a lingering doubt about what we were doing. Anette Debar had started it and Angie had pushed it further and I couldn't rid myself of it, this thought that we had taken a thinking, partially human animal and we were about to send it off to permanent captivity.

Sure, I knew what the money meant to us, to me. I could see on the faces of Mama and Papa what it meant.

And then Tebbetts had thought that blackfish

wanted to be around humans, and Doc had said, or I thought he said, that animals were often better off in zoos.

My head was beginning to feel like it was in the middle of a vise. But the tightening really hadn't even begun.

18

I stayed behind at Wilwilli to "guard" Tyrannus, as if he needed it, when Papa, Mama, Doc Greenlee, and Georgie Tebbetts went to Lumber Landing at about six. Not long after I heard the whir and flap of the chopper as it looped up toward Wilwilli. It circled twice around the cove, Zachary Cooke waving down at me, then went on south again to land down by the old cannery. Maybe twenty minutes later it took off again for Port Hardy.

Quiet settled over Wilwilli except for the whooshes, the bird cries, and now and then the cross-talk between the whales. Desdemona and Persephone hadn't gone away from the nets for more than two hours at a time since we'd caught Tyrannus. Doc Greenlee said they'd departed only to feed. Although killers will eat dead fish, as Tyrannus had done, they prefer live ones. Actually, for feasting, they prefer red mammal meat, Doc Greenlee said. Humpty whales or grays or seals or even close members of their own family, the playful dolphins.

Once, when Desdemona and Persephone were near South Rock, on the surface, Tyrannus came up. They talked to each other for a few seconds, and I swear to this day that they exchanged looks. The eyes of Tyrannus lit up when he saw his lovers. I'm positive of that. Then all three killers sank beneath the surface to talk in private through their "melons."

Again, what were they talking about? The predicament of Tyrannus? The weather? Fat salmon? A minke whale to chew on? Love talk?

It would have been pretty simple to make up my mind if I'd been able to buzz and creak and chatter like they did: "Okay, Ty, old buddy, do you want to live the rest of your life in a tank in show business or do you want to go back up off the Queen Charlottes? You want freedom?"

And if he whistled and up-screamed and down-screamed: "Hey, give me a break. That tank sounds good to me. I won't have to hunt for food. I'll have medical care until I die. I'll have some fun learning tricks. I can practice human speaking . . ." then I'd know what to do.

After a while, he came cruising near South Rock, a soft brown eye looking at me. I'd spent more time at Wilwilli than anyone else and I think by now that the blackfish recognized me. I could never prove it, but it seemed that way. He certainly wasn't ignoring me.

I went over to the wet burlap bags under which we'd stored some salmon and picked up a chunky one, tossing it into the water near Tyrannus. He wasted no time in gulping it down. Then I worked up some courage and took one to the water, holding it in the air until he swam over. Putting his white lower jaw on the edge of the rock, he waited until I dropped it. The fish vanished but he stayed, as if he wanted companionship.

I could just barely see his right eye. The look he gave me was curious, not frightening. It was a friendly look, and then a sound came from the blow-hole. It wasn't that rusty-hinge warning sound that Tebbetts had talked about. I thought it sounded like a human "hmm" and he did it twice.

I reached out and patted the huge shining black head. It was like thick rubber, as Angie had said. Like touching a smooth wet tire.

I felt a thrill like I'd never felt before. Here he was, twenty-five feet long, eight tons of wild animal, and he'd allowed me to touch him. Sure, Angie had done it, not thinking it was possible, and Tebbetts had done it, knowing it was possible, but this was me, J. W. Tidd. I'd done it! I'd overcome that killing of the humpty. I was laughing by that time. I'd done it!

Reaching over, I rubbed him two or three more times, almost scrubbing that giant rubbery skull. The "hmm" sound came again, maybe thanking me, and then he backed off, submerging. The great dorsal fin glided back to the center of the cove.

Sitting down, since my knees had gotten a little weak, I couldn't get over what had just happened. I guess it would be like making friends with a tiger, meeting him for the first time, touching him.

I was still afraid of the blackfish, of all that power and those jaws, but I thought I could now be friends with him. I thought he would let me be friends with him.

Soon, Papa came back with the *Dawn Girl,* and as soon as he had shut down the Volvo he said, proudly, "Look at these pitchers I shot."

I couldn't wait to tell him what had happened, but he was all wound up about the photos.

"Look," he said.

Zachary Cooke was right. They *were* sensational. Three or four showed Tyrannus all the way out of the water, spray flying off his body, just as I'd seen it. In one you could see him way up in the air, then the two females hanging on the humpty's mouth like leeches. The humpback's head was eight or ten feet out of the water.

"How about that?" Papa said. "I just pushed the button, that's all. I guess I went into the wrong profession. I made five hundred jus' for pushin' a button. I'll give up fishin' an' jus' shoot pitchers." He laughed and nodded, so pleased with himself.

I said, "They're great, Papa, and I have something to tell you now."

"What?"

"I petted the blackfish while you were gone."

Startled, a look of alarm on his face, he said, "You're kiddin' me."

"No, I'm not. I did it. He came right up here and put his head on the rock and I petted it."

"Jamie, are you plumb crazy? Jus' because that trainer can do it doesn't mean you can. He knows how. You don't. Don't you ever touch that fish again. You could've got killed here."

I shook my head. "He wants to be friends."

"Jus' listen to me. Feed him but keep away from him. You understand?"

I'd thought he'd be proud of me. Feeling let down, I said, "Let me tell you how it happened."

"I don't want to hear, an' don't you dare tell your mama. She's jittery enough after lookin' at those pitchers."

"He's two different animals, Papa. One out there in the sound, a different one in here."

Papa said, "Har-de-har," and closed the subject.

As we ate supper, some canned corned-beef hash and hot bread, Papa said, chewing away, "The plans are these. It'll take 'em about ten days to build that sea pen out of steel bars an' oil drums—it'll be about sixty feet long an' forty wide, with a catwalk aroun' the top. Then they'll come back an' get the blackfish. So we'll have him another two weeks, give or take a day or two. All we have to do now is feed him an' keep him happy. . . ."

I nodded. I'd try to do that. Feed him, of course. Nail a stiff brush to the end of a pole and scrub his back like Tebbetts did. Try talking to him in beeps and squeals and up-screams and down-screams. Communicate with him. And when Papa went away, as he'd have to do every few days, I'd pet that blackfish again, have that same thrill again.

Papa said, "Mr. Cooke gave me ten of those pretty hundred-dollar bills to buy sockeye." He made a funny face. "Hope I don't get used to spendin' hundred-dollar bills." Papa was in financial heaven, at last.

I was wishing he'd quit calling Cooke "Mister." There was something about that movie producer I didn't like or trust. "He didn't pay you everything?"

"Nope. Said he'll give me a check the day they start towin' the whale away." Papa suddenly laughed. "Wait'll I walk into the Bank of Vancouver with a hundred thousand dollars. Somethin' else I thought of. Soon as we get to Prince Rupert, I'm buyin' a new truck. Up there, we got to have wheels."

We hadn't had a pickup since we lived in Vancou-

ver, of course. The Dodge we had then was twenty
years old and needed a lot of nursing.

Though it was past nine, there was still more than
an hour of daylight left and we sat on the rock watching the killer whale move around in the cove.

Papa said, "I've never paid much attention to these
fish until now, 'cept to shoo 'em away."

"Not a fish, Papa," I said.

"Well . . ."

"Sometimes he seems almost human."

Papa grunted. "Not with those teeth."

I said, "I wish you'd been here to hear Doc Greenlee
say how human they were."

Papa laughed. "I saw how human they are when
he"—Papa nodded his head toward the black—"went
after that humpty. Jamie, a bear is a bear and a blackfish is a blackfish and don't let nobody mix 'em up in
your mind. Dogs sometimes act a little human, but
they are still dogs."

"Well, these dolphins are different, Doc Greenlee
said. So did Georgie Tebbetts." And now I knew they
were.

"Jamie, you and I fish for a living and it's better we
don't get ourselves all lathered up with these scien-
tific things. We got enough trouble with the government on days we can fish, days we can't. Why, these
damn environmentalists would like to have us burn
our gillnets. But you know what, Jamie? They'll go
into that fancy Empress Hotel tonight, order char-
coal-broiled fish an' a twenty-dollar bottle o' wine an'
think only about their bellies. Not a thought about the
rain an' cold to get that fish. Never a word about how
tough it is to make a livin' out here. Never a word
when a boat goes down an' men are lost. They yell

and holler when the Japs and Russkis go after whales,
but they keep dead silent when the Japs and Russkis
come right up to our doorstep an' clean us out o' fish."

I stayed quiet, knowing better than to argue when
he got into that kind of dark mood.

He watched our whale for a few minutes and then
turned to me, smiling now, his sudden anger tamped
down again. "It's been a good day, son. Time for me
to sleep. Just remember what I said aboot stayin'
away from this fish. G'night." He climbed aboard the
Dawn Girl.

I sat on the rock awhile longer, until it was dark,
watching Tyrannus and hearing the females talk to
him. Then I went into the tent and rolled around in
that sleeping bag, trying to sort things out. It wasn't
easy.

19

*E*arly evening of the third day after Zachary
Cooke, Doc Greenlee, and Georgie Tebbetts flew off to
Port Hardy to start work on the steel-lattice sea cage,
I was in the kitchen waiting for Mama to put our
supper into a thermos box when Angie burst through
the door, almost taking it off.

"Turn your TV on," she shouted, running over to hit
the switch. "You're on the satellite!"

"What are you talking about, Angie?"

The news channel came wobbling on and then
cleared but it was about the Middle East. That again.
Angie said, "Key-rap! You missed it."

Mama said, "We're on what channel, about what?"

Angie said patiently, spacing it out so we wouldn't
misunderstand, "One of those pictures was on the
news a minute ago—the blackfish way up in the air,
over the humptyback—and the commentator said
that the whale had been captured on the B.C. coast by
a fisherman named Tidd."

"Are you making that up, Angie?" I asked, sounding
accusing, I'll admit.

"No, I'm not," she snapped, suddenly angry. "He

also talked about a movie studio buying Tyrannus for exhibition." When she got angry little white lines formed along the bridge of her nose. They had formed.

Maybe she *was* telling the truth? "Honest? About us?"

"Did he say Perry Tidd shot that picture?" Mama asked excitedly. "Just wait until Per hears this. Just wait."

"I'm not sure. But he definitely said Perry Tidd had captured the whale. I don't think he said who shot the picture."

"How about me?" I asked.

"Nothing about you," Angie replied, with a hint of satisfaction.

"How did that get on TV?" Mama asked, looking baffled.

"Papa sold those pictures, remember?"

Mama suddenly hugged herself. "Yeah, for five hundred smackeroos." Mama had been acting almost giddy the last three days.

Angie said, "So that movie producer must have given the pictures to TV and told them about the blackfish."

I began switching channels, hoping to find the story, but it was past six-thirty and news usually didn't come up again until ten, unless there was a bulletin of some kind. Papa's photo of that blackfish on TV and here we'd missed it. Maybe in his whole lifetime this would never happen again.

I said to Mama, "He should come on back here and wait for the ten o'clock news."

"Yes, he should, Jamie." Though she moaned and groaned about living at Lumber Landing, and making a living off the sea, she really cared about my father. She loved him deeply, I knew.

I said, "I'll take the boat on up and then he can bring it back." Papa did not like to walk any farther than the floats. I don't think he'd ever been on the trail to Wilwilli. In fact, I don't think he'd ever walked up along the Lumber River trail.

Mama beamed. "He can eat with me while he waits here," she said, and went about taking his supper out of the thermos box.

Angie said, "I'll go up with you."

That was okay with me.

So I took the *Dawn Girl* on back to the cove, Angie as passenger, and told Papa what had happened. Standing on South Rock, holding the boat by its starboard rail, he thought I was kidding him. Angie straightened him out, saying she'd seen the photograph and heard his name.

"Honest?" he asked, unable to believe it.

"Honest," said Angie.

When I think back about the three weeks of Tyrannus, I think of many things, and the memories will never leave me. How Papa was like a big kid at a birthday party, shaking his head on opening presents he never dreamed of.

"My name on TV? Perry Tidd?" he said, eyes widening, the smile starting at his mouth and shoving aside the sun and wind lines. "My pitcher on TV?"

"The picture you shot," Angie said.

"Mama wants you to come on back, have supper, and wait for the ten o'clock news," I said.

Papa jumped aboard as we jumped off. "I might not get back tonight, Jamie," he shouted, still grinning.

"That's okay," I yelled back. My folks were seldom

alone in that small house now that I was their year-round boarder. They needed a vacation from me, and Mama could "work" on Papa about leaving the sea.

Papa made a tight turn and headed for Lumber Landing wide open, white water churning under that old boat. Fitz Hugh was like polished glass that clear evening, and the track of the *Dawn Girl* put a V in it that seemed to widen forever. The roar of the diesel shocked the peace.

The whales began talking as soon as the engine noise faded, and Angie said, "I'm sure that's love talk."

Oh, my, I thought. Here we go.

We were gracing South Rock, as usual, a monument nearly level except for two big cracks, one of which held the net anchor. By now I knew almost every inch of it. Angie sat in the wooden chair I'd brought up for Doc Greenlee.

Love talk, huh?

The two females were lingering by the net, and Tyrannus was on the cove side, of course, three or four feet from them, like a goldfish mashing his nose against an aquarium wall. I already knew that the experts could not tell if this particular clicking and buzzing was love talk. But it was pure Angie Pinheiro, the D.B. psychic, to interpret it that way. Three clicks and a buzz means "Kiss me, my darling." Then those black and white heads, the size of oil drums, would come together. Did they touch tongues?

Angie said, "I'll bet that almost every animal has a mating call."

Unromantic me, on most occasions, I said, "They could be talking about the weather."

She looked me straight in the eyes. "Have you ever been in love, Jamie?"

"Yes," I said, without wavering the slightest.

"With whom?"

Had a buffalo gun been lodged up against my crooked teeth, I wouldn't have told her. "A girl," I said. Dammit all, you!

"Well, that sounds normal. Did you ever tell her how you felt?"

"No, I didn't." And I might never.

"That's your hang-up. But these blackfish don't have that, I'm positive. They are saying exactly how they feel."

I wasn't going to argue. In a case like this, I've learned by now, when a woman gets into love talk there is no way to match it. Nor is there any way to win. Nodding—which doesn't necessarily mean yes— and keeping your eyes elsewhere is best. They beat you down if you go pupil to pupil. With her, it was a game I wouldn't have minded losing. I said, "Maybe."

Out on the ocean horizon, far beyond Hecate and Nalau islands, were some sun domes, yellow light that came down into the sea because the cloud cover was apparently thinner out there. These gold domes were sometimes in the summer sky when there was a drape of clouds on the horizon. I studied them.

"Did I ever tell you about Severa?"

"No." Severa who?

"Well, Severa was a very beautiful lady who sang the *fado* in Lisbon. A wonderful, handsome noble-man was in love with her, ready to give her the world at her feet, but she liked only bullfighters and thieves. A very sad story."

That was like the nun in the convent who wrote all

those letters. Didn't these Portuguese love affairs ever have happy endings?

"Severa is still mourned by all the *fadistas*. They wear black in her honor."

Fado, I had learned in our one-sided talks of a year ago, was an ancient way of singing, with guitars in the background. Angie had played a *fado* tape for me. She'd said, "It is a call from the heart."

It sounded to me like a bunch of hoarse wailing.

"Some brides get married in black, but not because of Severa."

I said, "Oh," still scanning the sun domes.

"In fact, I plan to get married in the black velvet dress that my grandmother wore when she was a bride. It is embroidered in silver. I'll carry a bouquet of fresh orange blossoms."

She was softening me up for something, I could tell.

"Jamie."

"What?" I turned to look at her. Yes, she'd be beautiful in black velvet with silver trimmings. She'd be the most beautiful bride that ever walked an aisle.

With a face so serious it could have belonged to Mary of the Purification, or any other Virgin Mary, she asked, "Have you thought about what I said—turning Tyrannus loose to join his lovers?"

Of course I'd thought about it. Could I? Should I? How? When? What would happen if I did? And did I really want to do it? I answered, "He's not going to be turned loose. Not by me, not by you, or anyone else. We *need* that money, Angie." I looked back at the horizon.

Studying me, she said, "It has to be done, you

know." She was working on me with those big, liquid eyes, trying to dent me. She put a hand on mine.

I kept silent.

"You know, you're keeping those babies in the bellies of Desdemona and Persephone away from their father."

Oh, Lord Almighty. Her new, clever tactic was now to make me feel guiltier. I said, "Doc Greenlee just guessed that they might be pregnant. He doesn't know. There's no test that he can make out here. And those babies, if they exist, could belong to five other blackfish."

Angie said, "We can do it, and your papa will never know. I'll get my survival suit out of the *Funchal,* go down, cut a big hole in the net, and your papa'll think Tyrannus did it."

I shook my head. "Angie, you know as well as I know that Papa can tell when a net has been cut. And that's beside the point. I'd never do that to my parents."

"I'll do it," she said. "You just look the other way."

I said, "Angie, you saw Papa a minute ago. Smiling, wasn't he? Happy, wasn't he? Not all full of worry about meeting bills and buying food. And Mama has been floating around that house for a week, so high she might never come down. She talks about going to Hawaii but I know she's really thinking about us starting a new life in Prince Rupert, about Papa leaving the boats. I've never seen them happier. That blackfish belongs to us. We caught him. We don't tell you and your papa what to do when you get a fish in your net."

Angie said, "Well, I'm sticking up for those babies.

Any decent female would do that. It's in our genes. You wouldn't know."

"I guess not," I replied. Then I added, "But your new tactic won't work."

Sort of offhanded, not really threatening me, she said, "We'll see."

Then she shifted the subject to her next to youngest sister, Isabel, who had married a potter and was living in Victoria. Isabel had sent her a tape by Fernando Maria, of Lisbon, a famous *fado* singer, unaware that Angie didn't play *fado* unless she was in a special mood.

Then she shifted the subject again—to that night up in Prince Rupert when she walked around the ledge four stories up. "I had on pajamas, I wasn't naked," she confessed. Another of the great disappointments in my life. I was wishing she hadn't told me the truth.

Angie soon walked home through the woods and Papa never did come back that night. Once again I spent some of it listening to whale talk and not much of it sleeping. One minute I'd be saying to myself, Turn him loose. The next, I'd be saying, I can't, I can't, I can't.

20

*M*idmorning of the next day, which stayed battleship gray from dawn to dusk, Papa and I were sitting out by the tent playing checkers, which he loved and I barely tolerated, when we heard the thrashing of a chopper and looked southwest. There was one headed up Fitz Hugh toward us.

Papa said, "I guess those Hollywood people are coming back. Wonder why?"

He was puzzled. There hadn't been enough time to build the sea cage and there'd been nothing on the radio, which we were always monitoring, to tell us they needed to visit again.

We stood up and waited as the bird came flap-flapping in and then saw "BC News" painted on the side in red. This chopper was from the British Columbia Broadcasting System. A door was open on one side and a camera aimed out.

Papa shouted, "They're gonna photograph us for TV. Wave at 'em, Jamie."

I did, and he scrambled over across South Rock to the *Dawn Girl* to get a salmon out of the hold. That would bring Tyrannus to the surface, of course. He was already programmed by nature to rise for the occasion, and Papa was now wise to the needs of TV. This was suddenly Hollywood for us Tidds. Papa was laughing, so pleased with himself.

The chopper came down lower, whipping up the surface of the cove, and sent wind waves back into the trees. I could see the cameraman aiming at us. Another man was standing in the opening, waving at us and nodding when Papa jumped back on South Rock with a whopping sockeye by the tail.

With all that noise and wind, I thought maybe Tyrannus would decline the offer, but he surfaced, sticking his head out about three feet. Papa, hamming it up, moved the fish higher so that the whale had to pump more with his flukes, keeping his head up longer.

Finally, Tyrannus got the fish and the black and white snout disappeared again.

The cameraman then seemed to concentrate for a few minutes on Desdemona and Persephone but they didn't cooperate. They were near the net and probably could be seen overhead but didn't break water for BC News.

The chopper moved sideways fifty or sixty feet and filmed the *Dawn Girl*, the rocks, and the net. Then the lens was aimed down at the tent. They covered everything at Wilwilli except the latrine we'd dug out in the timber.

Finally they came in close and the man just to the left of the cameraman waved his hand up and down, telling us, I think, to wave back. We did, with big toothpaste grins.

Then he gave us a salute, as if to thank us, and the chopper dipped away, then gained altitude and headed back in the direction from which it had come, roughly Vancouver Island.

With all that commotion and attention, I found myself pushing away all those doubts. Why, we were going to be famous. Suddenly it seemed all too big to even think about turning it around, letting the blackfish loose. Never had a TV helicopter been to visit Lumber Landing. It was absolutely show-business time for us in remote Fitz Hugh Sound.

Papa said, "Well, what about that?" He stepped over to the *Dawn Girl*, called Mama on the CB, and said, "Hey, we're TV stars now. A chopper came out from BC News to photograph us. Stayed here a good ten minutes, jus' hoverin' around."

Mama said, "We all heard that thing and wondered what it was doing. BC News, of all things."

Papa said, "It came in real close and that camera was right in our faces. I'll see if I can get Charlie an' let him know." Charlie was Papa's younger brother, living down in Vancouver.

Mama laughed merrily and said, "Let them all know. Yukaloo."

Papa signed off and we went back to our game of checkers, but it was hard to concentrate. Once he got up to call Mama and tell her to start monitoring every BCBS news show. I wasn't interested in winning, anyway.

About five o'clock he could stand it no longer and made a decision. "We're goin' back for the news programs. This fish'll be all right for an hour or so." He'd fed Tyrannus about four and the whale was asleep, floating on the surface, blowhole slightly awash, water slipping in to be whooshed gently out.

"He'll be fine," I said. Angie was at sea and I really

didn't think she was serious about cutting the nets. Nobody else at the Landing entertained such ideas, as far as we knew. Some of the fishermen might be a little jealous, but Papa was well liked on the floats.

We checked the nets and anchors, started the Volvo, and headed home.

Papa said, "If they'd told us they were comin', I woulda shaved this mornin'." Usually he gave shaving no particular thought. A week might go by without him touching a razor.

I might have worn a different jacket myself. I had a blue and red Enduro that would have looked great. Thinking ahead to the fall and school in Prince Rupert, I could hear them saying, "Oh, you're the guy from Lumber Landing, the one with the big blackfish. We saw you on TV."

Show-biz time.

I said, "I'm surprised Cooke hasn't called us." No word from him for four days.

"Well, he must be pleased with all this publicity. I guess they're busy building that sea cage. That's a lot o' weldin'. They're usin' the same kind of steel bar they use in house foundations, about a half inch round. I can't wait to see it. Doc Greenlee said they'd tow it at about four knots an' the whale will swim right inside it."

"Suppose he doesn't want to swim in there?"

"He won't have much choice, will he?"

"Think those females'll follow him right to Vancouver?"

"May well."

Mama must have been by the window because she came running down to the float to meet us when we laid the *Dawn Girl* alongside. Glowing, she said,

"Magnum, P.I., and his son." Mama was a Tom Selleck fan.

"I didn't know he had a son," said Papa, shutting down the Volvo.

Arm in arm, we went home for the grand and glorious debut of the Tidds on TV.

The news went from South Africa, where there'd been another riot, to Warsaw, where the Poles were complaining about another jump in meat prices, to Washington, where Congress was again fighting about military spending, to Montreal and Winnipeg and Quesnel, where there'd been a landslide, and finally, in closing, to Vancouver, where the commentator said, "We have a whale of a story for you tonight."

Papa said, "This is it!"

As the screen filled with a picture of Wilwilli Cove, the commentator said, "Here in remote Wilwilli Cove, more than a hundred miles north of Vancouver Island, in Fitz Hugh Sound, a huge killer whale is being held hostage."

I didn't like the way he said that, though it was true. *Held hostage!* He was telling people we were doing something wrong. We were kidnappers.

"It has been bought by a Hollywood movie studio, if one can 'buy' a killer whale, for exhibition at a new theme park in Southern California—where else? The whale has been named Tyrannus by one-time B-picture actor and now film producer Zachary Cooke, head of the new Ocean Arena. . . ."

The picture on the tube now included the *Dawn Girl,* Papa, and myself. We were on South Rock, looking up.

Mama shouted, "There you are, big as life!"

"The captors are a B.C. fisherman, Perry Tidd, and his son, Jamie, and Tyrannus is being held behind gillnets, which environmentalists always claim take a heavy toll of whales, seals, and dolphins. . . ."

Papa said loudly, "That's a damn lie!"

It wasn't altogether a lie.

"B.C. News has also learned that Tyrannus will not attack the nets because he doesn't realize that he can easily push them aside. The whale is being fed several hundred pounds of salmon every other day and soon faces the prospect of being airlifted to California, where he'll live out the rest of his days—maybe fifty years—in a small tank. It is believed he is the first killer whale to be captured in these waters in ten years. Greenpeace and other environmental organizations have waged a campaign against such captures for more than a decade."

Some footage of Papa feeding Tyrannus came on.

"And there is also a certain poignancy here at Wilwilli Cove because two smaller whales, which did not surface but can be seen below"—the picture changed again—"have stayed close to the nets since Tyrannus was trapped more than a week ago. An expert said that there is a probability that they are females, companions to Tyrannus, perhaps pregnant."

Ouch!

The screen then filled with a picture of widely smiling Zachary Cooke outside Port Hardy Inn.

"Cooke told B.C. News that it is likely that Tyrannus is the largest killer whale ever captured and that his company's investment will be something over three hundred fifty thousand, U.S., by the time Air Canada flies the huge animal south in a sheepskin hammock. Meanwhile, the fisherman and his son will be a hundred thousand dollars richer, as long as they can hang on to their hostage. This is John Royalton, Vancouver."

As the part about us being "a hundred thousand dollars richer" was being said, the screen filled with Papa and myself grinning and waving at the camera, as if we'd overheard what the commentator was saying. It made us look greedy. But we'd been encouraged to grin and wave by one of the men in the helicopter.

We sat there in total silence. I thought we'd be jumping up and down, laughing and carrying on. It was *the way* that the TV people had put things that hurt. You would have thought we were holding Black Beauty for ransom or had set Smokey Bear on fire.

Stunned, Mama was the first to speak. "He made you sound ugly, Per."

"I think it's called slanting the news," said a downcast Papa. His face was gray.

Mama said, "I wish we hadn't turned it on."

I said to them, "Let's turn him loose."

Papa looked at me and answered, grimly and flatly, "No!"

Mama echoed him. "Jamie, I'll say it again. We need that money. To hell with John Royalton." She seldom swore.

Papa got up tiredly. "The quicker that fellow Cooke comes an' gets that blackfish the better off we'll all be."

"Isn't that the honest truth?" Mama said.

We had a subdued supper and then went back to Wilwilli. Nothing had changed there. Tyrannus was still safe in the cove and the ladies were outside it, as usual.

Not much was said from then on, either. Papa was hurt. We used nets to trap fish and only occasionally did we ever get a seal or porpoise. It was the last thing we wanted to see in the meshes. They ripped and tangled nets trying to get loose. The B.C. News made it sound as if we purposely went after seals.

Papa's face told a lot that twilight. The light in it had suddenly dimmed down if not died.

21

I guess we should have known what was coming next—a gale of wind from the south, blowing up suddenly, carrying with it waves we'd never before encountered, even in January.

Papa was what he was, a licensed fisherman struggling to make a living. We obeyed all the rules, never dropping a net in a restricted area, fishing only on days that the government allowed. We always threw the little ones back if they were alive. Papa had yet to shoot a seal or porpoise entangled in our nets. He got them out and took the loss. Papa always preached and practiced conservation in the fishery.

And I'd always thought we were good people, not greedy ones. Sure, Mama wanted to leave Lumber Landing forever and get us off the sea. Papa wanted a new boat and a move to Prince Rupert, and I wanted a dirt bike and regular school. Was this being a "greedy fisherman," as an editorial in the Seattle paper said?

It was Doc Greenlee who got patched through at noon of the next day and his scratchy voice came on the radio to say, "All hell has broken loose halfway around the world over the whale. It was on all the networks yesterday, probably in all the newspapers. There's a Greenpeace group that's going to picket Oceans and Fisheries, the government agency in Victoria, another one in Seattle that's going to picket a distribution office of that movie company, and there's one down in California that's going to picket their studio in Hollywood. . . ."

Genuinely mystified, Papa asked, "For what?"

"Free the whale, that's what. They're getting signs painted up, 'Free Tyrannus.' And, Perry, don't be surprised if they send a boat right to Wilwilli Cove to picket you. There'll be a TV camera plane following it, without much doubt."

"Picket me? For what reason?" The look on Papa's face was disbelief.

"Their cause will play like Super Bowl on the six o'clock news."

"What about those other blackfish, the ones they already have swimmin' in tanks? There's at least one down at Sealand, in Victoria."

"Perry, there's at least thirty in captivity. They got 'em in California, got 'em in Ohio, Florida, Texas . . ."

"Well, then, what's all the picketing about?"

"Times have changed. These people want to stop *all* captures from now on, and you just happen to have the biggest one known to man."

That white oblong of plastic mike, in Papa's right hand, with its coiled extension cord to the side-band, was in danger of being crushed or ripped out. A vein in his neck was pulsing. He said, in a grim voice, "I'll shoot at any boat that comes near these nets."

Doc Greenlee's laugh was hollow. "I sympathize

wholeheartedly, but that wouldn't be a good idea. In fact, those people would love it. That would really play on the six o'clock news. Perry, you've stumbled into a hot one. Which animals can we capture for our own enjoyment? You're about to be hit over the head with animal rights."

Papa shouted, "Why is it that they don't say a damn word about the Russians an' Japanese robbin' us o' eatin' fish fifteen miles off this coast? Why don't they show pitchers of those big mother ships right under our noses? We're bein' ruined, whole families bein' destroyed, because the Russkis an' Japs are over-fishin' the whole ocean. Where are *those* pickets?"

Doc Greenlee said, quietly, "I agree, Perry, but I can't answer your question. I'll keep in touch. Georgie said to say hello to all of you. Regards to Mrs. Tidd."

"Where is Cooke in all this?" Papa asked.

Again, Doc Greenlee's laugh was a little hollow. "He went back to Hollywood yesterday. Told us to keep working on the sea cage. Said he'd be back tomorrow."

Doc signed off.

Papa turned away from the radiotelephone and sat down heavily on the high stool, seeming to shrink. He blinked and shook his head. "I'm not sure what to do." He looked bewildered. He could face twenty-five-foot seas but didn't know how to handle TV commentators and Greenpeace people and the Zachary Cookes and the meanings of the words they said.

He sat on the stool for a while, looking off to sea, the place that he knew so well. I said nothing, realizing he was thrashing around up in his head. Then he got up slowly and tiredly, stepping off the *Dawn Girl* onto South Rock. He stood there, again in silence, just watching the whale. I went over beside him and watched, too, almost wishing none of this had ever happened.

Finally, he said, "I've made up my mind, Jamie. They can say all those words they want about us but I'm not backin' down. We're fishermen an' we caught this blackfish fair an' square. He's ours to sell."

Then he did something he seldom did. He pulled me close, his hard hand gripping my shoulder. I could feel both the strength and anger.

Papa did know how to handle picket boats without any doubt at all. If they came toward the nets, that shark rifle strapped up on the ceiling would bark a few times.

22

I saw Angie the next morning about ten o'clock over by the float. She was hosing down the *Funchal*, water sloshing down the deck and spilling out through the scuppers. Between the pound of the pumps and the water splash, she didn't know I was there until I shouted at her.

She dropped the brass nozzle to the deck and yelled, "I heard about TV last night."

"Yeah. They made us look like mean jailkeepers."

"Well, Jamie," she said. She stepped inside the pilothouse to stop the engine. "That's what you're doing, keeping that whale in prison, isn't it? Hostage? How else do they say it?"

"Come on, Angie. We're doing it for someone else. We don't want that blackfish ourselves. We're just keeping him temporarily. Just to earn some money. You know that."

"You're as guilty as that ham actor." She could hurt you at times. Hurt you bad.

"Angie, as you already said, if your papa had come by Wilwilli before we did and saw that blackfish go into the cove, he would have trapped it."

"And I told you I would have protested him being a jailkeeper."

I said, "Angie, I don't want to argue with you. I'm not up to it. All we want to do is send that blackfish on its way, then Zachary Cooke can battle with all those Greenpeace people. B.C. News showed them marching outside Oceans and Fisheries, carrying signs. Doc Greenlee said they plan to send a picket boat."

She softened, as she always did. "I know," she said. "I feel as sorry for you as I do for those three whales. You got sucked into your own trap."

I said, "Angie, Papa has to go to Kwiklit this afternoon. If you're not doing anything, come on up to the cove. It gets lonely up there."

She said, "Okay," started the engine again, and finished up the hose-down. Nothing dirties a boat quicker than fish guts and dried scales.

The day could not have been prettier at Wilwilli. Plenty of blue sky and brilliant sunshine and the temperature was in the low seventies. It was the kind of day when Mama sat outside and pretended she was in the tropics. Not many days like that year-round.

The *Dawn Girl* pulled away from sunny South Rock a little after noon. Papa had to buy more fresh sockeye for Tyrannus at Kwiklit. At the rate that hungry whale was going, he'd eat up two thousand dollars' worth of salmon before Doc Greenlee and Georgie Tebbetts hauled him away in the sea cage.

Tyrannus was either snoozing or yapping to Desdemona and Persephone or fluking lazily around the cove. He seemed to be contented. It was entirely possible he was enjoying this lazy life, not having to swim all over the ocean for food. Of course we weren't giving him deluxe humptyback or minke meat, which he might have preferred.

To pass time, and get my mind off the TV broadcast, I'd brought along several catalogs to reread; Krause Racing and Moto-X Fox, as well as a paperback, *Championship Training* (for dirt hills), and took the borrowed air mattress out of the tent, carrying it over to South Rock, where I planned to spend a leisurely afternoon. I settled down about twelve-thirty.

There was one race I really wanted to do, the Barstow-to-Vegas run, one hundred fifty-five miles across desert from California to Nevada. Over a thousand riders bounced those saddles over mixed pavement and sand. For a dirt-bike rider, heat and dust, and the noise of rumbling banshees, it was like going to heaven on Pirellis.

I must have fallen asleep about two o'clock, and was deep into a Barstow-Vegas dream about thirty minutes later, when I awoke to a muffled scream and rolled over to see Angie, in her yellow survival suit, in the middle of the cove. For a split second I thought I was still dreaming. Crazy Angie, what was she doing out there in that waterproof suit? You wore those only if your boat went down.

Then I realized it wasn't a dream because she screamed again.

Tyrannus was beside her on the surface, one brown eye focused on her, and just as I got to my feet he took her left shoulder into his jaws, not crunching down on her, just holding, and did a slow-motion dive to the bottom.

Just before her head went under she saw me for a flash, her eyes wide and pleading, full of a horror that I still cannot describe to this day.

For a few seconds I was paralyzed, not so much from fear of Tyrannus, but from not knowing what to do. Days earlier, when I was alone on the rock, I'd thought about Georgie Tebbetts saying that he always wanted someone around with an oxygen flask in case a killer took him to the bottom. I didn't think about that at all now, and there was no oxygen around, anyway.

But Papa had put a dozen fat sockeyes under the wet burlap bag, to toss out now and then, and without really thinking beyond giving Tyrannus a choice of food, I grabbed a big one by the tail, kicked the others off, and dived in.

The icy water was like a sword cutting across my chest, and all breath seemed to be sucked out for a second or so, but I kicked on down the roughly ten feet to the bottom, spotting the mass of yellow beside that huge black and white barrel that was Tyrannus. The bright sun had lit up the water and there wasn't much sediment in it, the spring snow flood having come down much earlier.

The whale was belly-flat on the bottom and Angie was on her back, as if doing bicycle exercises, her feet up in the air, enclosed in the yellow suit, legs ballooned by air. Her long hair floated straight up toward the surface.

It was a weird scene, almost as if Tyrannus was saying, Well, I'm just going to hold you down here for a little while. I don't plan to eat you.

For maybe two seconds I saw her face in the band of light that angled from above. Bubbles were leaking from her nose and mouth as she tried to hold her breath. There was shock and terror in her eyes. I'll never forget that face, long hair drifting up from it.

I've seen it in nightmares several times, almost as if she was in a glass tank and I was outside looking in, thinking, Well, that's unusual.

I believe, but am not sure, that I pushed the salmon by his mouth and released it. Maybe it just came loose out of my hand. But I clearly remember seeing his right eye, which was about the size of a tennis ball, roll upward as the fish went by him. He seemed to think about it for a moment.

Then the jaws, with those murderous interlocking teeth, released Angie to go after a tastier snack.

I grabbed her hair and kicked upward. The survival suit, which had not even been pierced by his teeth, had a lot of air trapped in it and she bobbed up.

Afraid to look back and see where Tyrannus might be and what he was doing, I shoved her to the rock. Getting a toehold, I pitched myself out, still clinging to her. After heaving her to safety, with strength I never knew I had, I must have passed out for a few seconds. I know that I was out of breath and likely fainted. Whatever did happen, I wasn't out more than ten or fifteen seconds.

I remember that I came to and saw that she was safe on the rock. I crawled over. She was on her back, eyes closed, hair wrapped all around her neck and over her mouth. I pulled it away. Her face was grayish-white except for some slight blueness around the lips. She didn't seem to be breathing.

She'd zipped the survival suit up to her neck but hadn't pulled the hood over her head. The flotation pillow was still attached to the back of her neck. I unzipped her, jerked the suit down to her knees, freeing her arms, then knelt down facing her head and began rescue breathing, the way they'd taught me at the Port Hardy school.

Hand on her forehead, pinching her nose with my fingers, the other hand under her neck, lifting it to keep the airway open, I blew into her mouth until I saw her chest rise. Then I turned my head to the side to watch her chest for a falling movement and hear the air escaping. I gave her four deep breaths in rapid succession, then began the pattern of a single breath every five or six seconds.

I remember that I yelled at her between breaths, telling her how stupid she was, scared to death she was dead or would die.

Suddenly there was a gasp and water started coming up. I turned her head and she vomited. Oatmeal and water came up.

I kept up the rescue breathing until she was on her own, but she still wasn't conscious.

Now I'm told I should have stayed with her until help arrived, but I decided to run back to the Landing instead of waiting for Papa to return. She might die in the meantime, I thought. First, I made sure her tongue hadn't slipped down into her throat, then I checked to see where Tyrannus was. The dorsal fin showed up at the far end of the cove, but I still dragged Angie farther up on the rock, then started for home.

Why it was that I chose that time to break down and begin crying as I ran I'll never know. I could have waited until I got home. It doesn't make any difference. Cursing and bawling, I covered the slippery mile through the woods in maybe seven or eight minutes, or less, and pushed our door open, having trouble speaking. I looked a mess, still soaked to the skin.

But Mama finally understood that Angie had almost drowned at Wilwilli and had Dick Jahraus call for the Coast Guard to emergency-airlift her to a hospital. Then Dick called the *Dawn Girl* to tell Papa what had happened, to come straight to the Landing.

Finally we ran over to the Pinheiros' house to tell them. Cristovão was napping, usual on any afternoon he didn't fish, and in a few minutes we headed for the cove in the *Funchal*, wide open. Mrs. Pinheiro stayed home to man their CB.

On the way Cristo demanded to know why Angie had done such a "stoopid thing." Putting that survival suit on, getting in the water with the blackfish? He was suspicious of me. He kept staring at me as if I'd plotted the whole thing, filling the air with blue-white Portuguese.

Then Mama got fed up with that and yelled at him, "You idiot, if it wasn't for Jamie, Angie would be dead."

Cristo shut his mouth and a few minutes later the *Funchal* was alongside South Rock and I jumped off to tie the bow line up to our anchor stock.

Cristo leapt off the boat and went to Angie's side, knelt down, and began to sob, saying things in Portuguese. She looked dead, all right. She hadn't moved a quarter inch since I left her.

I felt numb.

Mama moved Cristo aside, slipping her hand under Angie's shirt and placing a finger under Angie's nose. Mama said, "She's alive, Cristo. Believe me, she's alive."

That only made the tough old Portogee fisherman cry harder.

I stood back, not knowing what else to do.

Mama yelled at Cristo again. "You got any blankets in there?" She motioned to the *Funchal*.

Still on his knees, he moaned and nodded, then lifted his head back to pray to the Virgin Mary. He was as useless as I was.

"Get them, Jamie," said Mama, taking command. "We have to move her back to the Landing."

There was not enough clearing at Wilwilli for a chopper to land and there was no sense in trying a basket-lift. Anyway, the chopper wouldn't arrive at the Landing for at least another half hour.

In a few minutes, after pulling the survival suit off, we wrapped her in blankets and then carried her aboard, Mama talking to her steadily and soothing her forehead along the hairline. There is nothing like a woman to do something like that.

Angie remained unconscious on the way home and Mama said, "What worries me is that she hasn't snapped out of it yet. She's in shock, of course, but some people just die that way."

I didn't want to hear that.

Her breathing seemed normal, but she appeared to be in a deep sleep. The blueness was gone from around her lips, and though she didn't have much color, the grayness was gone too.

Mama kept talking to her and then slapped her three or four times.

Old Cristo turned from the wheel to complain and Mama barked at him, "If you know better than I do, come here and Jamie'll take the wheel."

Again, Cristo retreated and shut up.

We reached the Landing about three forty-five. Papa was already there and helped Cristo carry Angie up to the cannery loading dock. We already knew that the helicopter was less than fifteen minutes away. The pilot had been reporting his position to the *Funchal*, checking in when he arrived over Calvert Island, saying that he had a doctor and nurse aboard.

About four o'clock the big yellow Labrador CH 46 chopper, of Squadron RCC 442, Transport and Rescue, at Comox, sat down but kept the tandem rotors going. The doctor, nurse, and medical aide lifted Angie into a gurney and carried her to the whirlybird. Cristo and the aircraft lifted off and churned south. They were bound for the hospital at Port Hardy. If necessary, a jet would then take her on to Vancouver.

"Okay, tell me what happened, Jamie," said Papa.

I told him everything that I remembered.

"Why did she do it?" he asked. "Get in there with that fish? Was she trying to prove something? Or is she just insane?"

I hesitated. I knew why, of course. I didn't see the knife in her hand, but I was sure it could be found on the bottom at Wilwilli.

Papa stared at me for a moment, angrily, then said, "Okay, Jamie, let's go on up there. Go with us, Lace."

23

As we passed out of the harbor and swung north, Papa said, insistently, "Why, Jamie?"

"She was going to turn Tyrannus loose. I think she had a knife and was going to cut a big hole in the nets, so it would look like he just busted through himself. She wasn't afraid of him and put on that survival suit so she could stay in the cold water for a while."

Papa broke in, with a metallic laugh, "She knows damn well I can tell when a net's been cut with a knife."

Sure, Papa, she knew that, I thought. However, I said, "But we wouldn't have known *who* knife-cut it."

Mama's laugh was brittle. That was ridiculous, too, the laugh said.

We all would have known instantly who cut the net. Nobody but crazy Angie! Nobody else in Lumber Landing would have been crazy enough to slide down into the water with a killer whale that wasn't at all trained.

"I don't see how she could be that bubble-headed," Papa said.

If he'd known that she'd walked around a ledge

four stories up in Prince Rupert, he might believe she was capable of swimming with a blackfish.

Papa shook his head. "She risked her life to cut the nets?"

Mama said, "I guess she's a lot deeper than we think, Per."

I'd had a question on my mind for the past half hour. "I wonder what would have happened if she'd worn a black suit like Georgie Tebbetts instead of yellow?"

Mama said, "I'm not going to waste any time trying to find out whether or not blackfish are color blind."

I said, "Tyrannus might not have paid any attention to her with black on. You know, I don't think he knew he was drowning her. He just took her to the bottom and held her. When his jaws closed on her shoulder it was very gentle. I saw it. And he let her loose after he saw the sockeye."

Papa sighed. "His mind is always on his belly. Remember the humpty, Jamie?"

"Papa, he's a lot more human than you think. Believe me!"

Papa looked at me strangely.

A few minutes later we got to Wilwilli and tied up. The only evidence that anything had happened in that lonely cove was the crumpled survival suit on South Rock. Otherwise, it was the same as it had been for days, Tyrannus coming up from the far end as humans again made an appearance, surfacing and blowing. Saying hello to people he knew? Waiting for a fish to be thrown his way? Waiting to have his back scrubbed? He did have a thinking brain, I was convinced. He knew us, all right.

Faithful Desdemona and Persephone hovered around their side of the net and, when he surfaced a second time, sent some whistles and clicks to him. He surged under in a streak of white water, then rose and whistled back to them. They *were* his lovers, I was now convinced. They *were* carrying his babies.

Then he swam close to South Rock, one big eye on us. I think I could have drowned in that eye. I'd never felt so guilty in my life.

He circled on out, then made another pass by us, looking, looking, looking.

Thinking of what Angie had been trying to do, thinking of her so still and white, so near death, I finally said to them, "You know, we have to turn him loose. We owe him something. He let me have Angie when she was on the bottom. He didn't harm me."

Without turning his head, Papa answered slowly, flatly, "No, Jamie, we're not turning him loose. If you hadn't been around, he would have killed her. Don't go makin' excuses for him."

Staring at the side of his blocky head, the thick neck, chin jutting out, red hair ruffling in the evening breeze, I knew that all his stubbornness had just surfaced again. That whale was a goner.

I shouted at him, *shouted*, "I wish she'd cut this rotten net, I wish I'd cut it!"

Mama said sharply, "Jamie . . ."

Still watching Tyrannus, Papa said, not raising his voice a decibel, "Son, this is a fish that swims in the sea, an' don't give me any crap about him havin' human ways. You got a short memory. He's stayin' here until Cooke collects him. Now, let's feed him an' be done with this talk."

I fought back tears on the way over to the *Dawn Girl*. Stepping on board, I opened the hatch and jumped down inside to the bed of ice that nestled the salmon.

24

*I*t was now a little after six and Mama was getting ready to walk back to Lumber Landing to fix our supper when the side-band awakened with the voice of Doc Greenlee calling the *Dawn Girl* from Port Hardy.

Papa acknowledged, and then Doc said, without warning, "It's all over, Perry."

"What's all over?"

"Cooke and that movie company knuckled under. Cooke just called me to say send him a bill for my services and tell Georgie to come home, stop work on that sea pen."

Stunned, Papa said, "I don't understand."

Mama looked over at me, frowning widely.

Doc said, "The pressure got too much for them, Perry. I thought it might. Those 'Free the Whale' people had more pickets out at the studio gates this morning. The TV and press people were making the movie company look bad. Greenpeace would have hounded the sea pen all the way to Vancouver. It was a no-win situation."

As if he couldn't believe that the hundred thousand

wasn't to be, Papa said, "It's all over?" I noticed that
his chin quivered slightly, first time I'd ever seen that.

" 'Fraid so," said Doc.

Face drained, Papa was silent a moment, then
asked, "What about us?"

Both Mama and I hung on every word.

Doc said, "I brought that up. Cooke said you knew
you were taking a gamble when you caught that
whale. He said he'd fed it and paid you five hundred
for those pictures. He said they were worthless to him
now."

"But I lost fishin' money while keepin' this whale
for him," Papa protested.

Doc said, "I know. Well, maybe you should think
about suing Cooke and the studio."

Papa's laugh was like chain rattling in the hawse
pipe. *Sue a movie studio in Hollywood?* This was
Lumber Landing, where we didn't even have electricity.

Doc said, "I'm sorry. I'll testify for you."

Papa took a deep breath and straightened his shoulders. He said, "Thanks, Doc. Tell Georgie Tebbetts
good-bye from us. Either of you up this way, drop in."

That wasn't very likely.

Papa signed off, turning to look at us.

Tears ringed my mother's eyes. Finally she said,
"You know, I think that Zachary Cooke wears a tou-
pee. It's a good one because you can't see where the
real hair leaves off and the phony hair begins. I've
never trusted men who wore toupees."

Despite how he was feeling, Papa had to laugh at
that. She could always make him laugh.

Yet it was her time to sigh and wipe at her eyes. "I

guess funny, skinny Lacy will have to wait awhile longer for Maui, Prince Rupert, and whatever."

In all the years I'd known him, I'd never seen Papa with even a trace of water in his eyes. It was there now. He sniffed and said, "Whipped again." Then he pulled us both into his massive arms and said, "We'll survive."

Mama said, fiercely, "Yes, we will."

It reminded me of that late twilight at Wilwilli Cove after we'd learned that Zachary Cooke wanted the whale, we three almost dancing around on the rock, ready to be fired off into space.

I hugged them tighter and echoed her. Another winter in Lumber Landing, though. Lordy.

Then Papa said to both of us, suddenly angry at the whole world, "I'm not letting him go because of Greenpeace or that lousy TV station or that movie actor. Believe that. They can take their high an' mighty ways an' all go to hell forever. I hope they do. But you got it right, Jamie. That blackfish traded you and Angie for his freedom. That's the kind of thing I respect, fish or man. You can tell everybody I said that."

"I will, Papa."

"An' you can tell everybody that we turned him loose before that movie actor notified me personally an' officially. He hasn't done that yet."

Mama nodded, fighting tears.

I said, "I will, Papa."

"Now, Jamie, let's get that net aboard. We'll need it in another day."

The sockeye were running fat and strong up at Koeye.

In a few seconds the Volvo roared.

So we took the anchor off South Rock and began pulling the monofilament net owned by the Bank of Vancouver into the *Dawn Girl.* It didn't take long, and then Tyrannus was free to leave Wilwilli, but before he could depart, Persephone and Desdemona rushed in to meet him.

Killer whales don't kiss is my uneducated guess, but these ladies did immediately what they knew would please a lover just out of jail. Making passes over and under him, they massaged his belly and back.

Watching, Mama said, "I've got a hunch that Doc Greenlee is right. Those ladies are carrying his babies."

We then dumped about three hundred dollars, U.S., in sockeyes, courtesy of Zachary Cooke, at the mouth of the cove and the three killer whales had a fine meal before starting on their journey to wherever that would be. Cooke owed us that and more.

We stayed off Wilwilli until they headed west, Desdemona and Persephone on either side of the huge killer whale known around the world as Tyrannus. The last we saw of that great dorsal fin, it was aimed for Hakai Passage, and beyond there, of course, was open ocean. Freedom.

As we started back for Lumber Landing, Papa called the marine operator and asked to be patched through to the hospital at Port Hardy. When that was done he asked the hospital switchboard to connect him to Angela Pinheiro's room.

In a moment the voice of old Cristo came up and Papa passed the mike to me.

I said, "Cap'n Pinheiro, this is Jamie Tidd, on the *Dawn Girl.* How is Angie? Over."

"Esshe's gonna be fine. Esshe's sleep now. Over."

I said, "When she wakes up, tell her we turned the blackfish loose. Tell her he went to sea with Desdemona and Persephone."

Cap'n Pinheiro answered, "Dessa-wot, an' Percee-wot? Over."

"She'll know."

Old Cristo was still hung up on Desdemona and Persephone. He said, "I no unnerstan Dessade. . . ."

I had to laugh. I knew I'd never have trouble from him again.

"Just tell her the blackfish is free. Free! Over and out from the *Dawn Girl.*"

A week later Angela Ione Pinheiro came home from Port Hardy on Farley McCoy's mail boat, the *Nootka.* This time it wasn't raining. The sun was brilliant and greenery shimmered all the way up the mountains above Lumber Landing.

Everyone turned out to welcome her and this time I didn't hang back. I was right in front when she stepped onto the float and I looked her straight in the eyes. I said, "I love you for what you did, and for who you are. . . ." I'd rehearsed that speech and, there, I'd said it.

Angie blinked, then threw her arms around me and hugged and hugged and hugged.

I was progressing.

Freedom

As black, starless night finally blotted out the horizon, the water pastures came alive with microscopic things that none of the killer whales could see. They surrounded the trio, luminous eyes in weirdly shaped bodies, some almost transparent—wandering animal and vegetable plankton but not interesting nor massed enough for a meal. They flowed around the rapidly swimming orcas like curds of jelly. Rolling, tumbling, washing, falling behind.

Larger shapes cruised the night, too, cutting frantic phosphorescent streaks on all sides of the small pod. Fish jumped and flopped back, chirping and screeching. The whole ocean was a sounding board and the orcas listened, and echo-ranged, ever vigilant for the hulk of a ponderous whale or some fat sockeyes.

The hunting prospects for the killer whale once called Tyrannus and his ladies were indeed excellent this early July as the flowers came into full bloom ashore.